# NORY RYAN'S
# SONG

*Also by Patricia Reilly Giff*
*in Large Print:*

Lily's Crossing

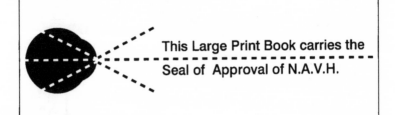

This Large Print Book carries the
Seal of Approval of N.A.V.H.

# NORY RYAN'S SONG

# Patricia Reilly Giff

**Thorndike Press • Waterville, Maine**

μμἶ

Published in 2001 by arrangement with Random House
Children's Books, a division of Random House, Inc.

Thorndike Press Large Print Juvenile Series.

The tree indicium is a trademark of Thorndike Press.

The text of this Large Print edition is unabridged.
Other aspects of the book may vary from the original edition.

Set in 16 pt. Plantin by Myrna S. Raven.

Printed in the United States on permanent paper.

**Library of Congress Cataloging-in-Publication Data**

Giff, Patricia Reilly.
 Nory Ryan's song / Patricia Reilly Giff.
  p.  cm.
  Summary: When a terrible blight attacks Ireland's potato
crop in 1845, twelve-year-old Nory Ryan's courage and
ingenuity help her family and neighbors survive.
  ISBN 0-7862-3459-8 (lg. print : hc : alk. paper)
  1. Ireland — History — Famine, 1845–1852 — Juvenile
fiction.  2. Large type books [1. Ireland — History —
Famine, 1845–1852 — Fiction.  2. Famines — Ireland
— Fiction.  3. Brothers and sisters — Fiction.
  4. Survival — Fiction.  5. Ireland — Emigration and
immigration — Fiction.  6. Large type books.]  I. Title.
PZ7.G3626 No 2001
[Fic]—dc21                                              2001027696

*For Anna Donnelly,*
*who stayed.*
*For the Reillys,*
*who sailed on the* Emma Pearl.
*For the Monahans,*
*who came to 416 Smith Street.*
*For the Haileys, the Cahills,*
*and the Tiernans,*
*who finally had that bit of land.*
*For all of them, my family.*


*For my children and grandchildren:*
*Jim, Laura, Jimmy, and Christine*
*Bill, Cathie, Billy, Cait, and Conor*
*Alice, Jim, and Patti . . .*
*a memory of* An Gorta Mór,
*the Great Hunger.*


*And most of all*
*for Jim.*

# Glossary

| | | |
|---|---|---|
| *a stór* | uh **stoar** | my dear |
| *bean sídhe* | ban-**shee** | female fairy beings who wail when someone is about to die |
| *diabhal* | **djow**-uhl | devil |
| *Dia duit* | **djee**-a-**ditch** | God save you (a greeting) |
| *fuafar* | **fu**-uh-fur | disgusting, hateful |
| *madra* | **mah**-druh | dog |
| *poitín* | **puh**-tjeen | an alcoholic drink made from potatoes |
| *Rith leat!* | **rih-leat** | Run away! |
| *sídhe* | shee | creatures from another world who sup posedly cause trouble |

# Chapter 1

Someone was calling.

"Nor-ry. Nor-ry Ry-an."

I was halfway along the cliff road. With the mist coming up from the sea, everything on the path below had disappeared.

"Wait, Nory."

I stopped. "Sean Red Mallon?" I called back, hearing his footsteps now.

"I have something for us," he said as he reached me. He pulled a crumpled bit of purple seaweed out of his pocket to dangle in front of my nose.

"Dulse." I took a breath. The smell of the sea was in it, salty and sweet. I was so hungry I could almost feel the taste of it on my tongue.

"Shall we eat it here?" he asked, grinning, his red hair a mop on his forehead.

"It'll be over and gone in no time," I said, and pointed up. "We'll go to Patrick's Well."

We reached the top of the cliffs with the rain on our heads. *"I am Queen Maeve,"* I sang, twirling away from the edge. *"Queen of old Ireland."*

I loved the sound of my voice in the fog, but then I loved anything that had to do with music: the Ballilee church bells tolling, the rain pattering on the stones, even the *carra-crack* of the gannets calling as they flew overhead.

I scrambled up to Mary's Rock. As the wind tore the mist into shreds, I could see the sea, gray as a selkie's coat, stretching itself from Ireland to Brooklyn, New York, America.

Sean came up in back of me. "We will be there one day in Brooklyn."

I nodded, but I couldn't imagine it. Free in Brooklyn. Sean's sister, Mary Mallon, was there right now. Someone had written a letter for her, and Father Harte had read it to us. Horses clopped down the road, she said, bringing milk in huge cans. And no one was ever hungry. Even the sound of it was wonderful. Brook-lyn.

The rain ran along the ends of my hair and into my neck. I shook my head to make the drops fly and thought of my da on a ship, the rain running down his long dark hair too. Da, who was far away, fishing to pay the rent. He had been gone for weeks, and it would be months before he came home again.

I swallowed, wishing for Da so hard I had to turn my head to hide my face from Sean. I blew a secret kiss across the waves; then we picked our way up the steep little path to Patrick's Well.

We sat ourselves down on one of the flat stones around the well and leaned over to look into the water. People with money threw in coins for prayers. But the well was endlessly deep, wending its way down through the cliffs toward the sea, and it took ages for coins to sink to the bottom. Granda said that might be why it took so long for those prayers to be answered.

But not many people had coins to drop into the well. Instead there was the tree overhead. People tied their prayers to the branches: a piece of tattered skirt, the edge of a collar.

"I see my mother's apron string." Sean pointed up as he tore a bit of dulse in two and handed me half.

I nodded, sucking on a curly edge. I looked up at the tree. A strip of my middle sister Celia's shift was hanging there. Now, what did that one want? She had no shame. There it was, a piece of her underwear left to wag in the wind until it rotted away. Every creature who walked by would be gaping at it.

I stood up quickly, moving around to the other side of the well to look down at our glen. The potato fields were covered with purple blossoms now, and stone walls zig-zagged up and down between.

And then, something else.

"Sean," I said, "what's happening down there?"

Absently he tore the last bit of dulse in two. "Men," he said slowly. "Bailiffs with a battering ram. Someone is being put out of a house."

Someone. I knew who it was. A quick flash of the little beggar, Cat Neely, her curly hair covering most of her face. And Cat's mother, who sat in their yard, teeth gone, cheeks sunken, with no money to pay the rent.

"Don't think about it," Sean said, his hand on my shoulder, his face sad. "There's nothing can be done."

"Coins," I said. "If only someone . . ." I broke off. I knew it myself. No one in the glen had an extra penny. Not Sean's family. Not mine. My older sister Maggie and Sean's brother Francey were saving every bit they could to get married. But even that would take years.

The dulse on my tongue tasted bitter now. Cunningham, the English lord, owned all our land, all our houses; he could put any of us out if he wanted. And now it would be Cat and her mother.

There was someone with a coin, I knew that.

Anna Donnelly.

Sean and I were afraid of her. He had said that one of the *sidhe* might live under her table. I shuddered, thinking of those beings from the other world. *Tangles of gray hair, bony fingers pointing, crouched in the darkness.* Anna had magic in her, too. She could heal up a wen on the finger, or straighten a bone with her weeds, but only when she wanted to.

And she hadn't saved my mam the day my little brother, Patch, was born.

That Anna Donnelly had a coin.

And I was the only one who knew about it.

I thought of the day I had stopped near her house. The thatch on her roof was old and plants grew green over the top. And there was Anna outside, teetering on a stool, her white hair in wisps around the edge of her cap. She had peered over her shoulder, her face as wrinkled as last year's potatoes, then held something up before she shoved it deep into the thatch.

I had seen the glint of it, the shine.

The coin.

And in my mind now: I could save Cat Neely and her mother. If only Anna would give me that coin.

Suddenly my mouth was dry.

I turned to Sean. "Thank you for the dulse," I said, and left him there, mouth open, as I flew down the path away from the cliff.

# Chapter 2

I hurled myself along the road, thinking about the bailiffs and Devlin, who collected the rents for Lord Cunningham. They'd tear down the roof of the Neely house and pound at the beam until it splintered in over the hearth. Nothing would be left but dust, and chunks of limestone, and bits of thatch settling on the floor.

Cat would be sobbing, her tiny face blotched, and her mother rocking back and forth outside, both of them with nowhere to go. Devlin would never let them stay with another family. "Lord Cunningham wants to clear this land," he'd say, "not add more faces to each house."

I crossed our own field, seeing my sister Maggie drawing a picture on the wall of the house. Three-year-old Patch was dancing around her. "Me," he was saying. "It's my face."

They didn't see me, and I didn't stop. What would I say to Anna? I wondered. *My da will be home soon, long before the rent is due,* I'd tell her. *We will give you back the coin straightaway. But right now we could save Cat and her mother.* Even the thought of knocking on her door dried my mouth and dampened my hands. But if she said yes I could bring the coin to Cat and put it into her little fist. When she opened her hand, her mother would see it.

I picked up my skirt and catercornered across Anna's field, one hand covering the stitch in my side. I could feel my fingers trembling. I went up the path then before I could change my mind, rapped hard on the door, and stepped back.

Nothing happened. I leaned forward and knocked again. The door stayed shut. Where was Anna? Where had she gone? Was someone's baby being born in one of the far glens?

From far away I heard the men shouting. I went out to the path to see if she was coming. *Please come, Anna Donnelly. Please.*

I turned and looked back at the thatch. The coin was right there. It was so close I could climb up and reach for it.

And then the door opened.

My hand flew to my mouth. I stepped back, so frightened I hardly remembered why I was there.

Anna stared at me with faded blue eyes, her head to one side.

I opened my mouth, but I couldn't speak.

She took a step outside, listening to the men shouting in the distance. "They are putting the Neelys on the road?" Her lips were puckered, with deep lines around her mouth.

"Lend me a coin for them," I said in a rush. "I will pay you."

"And how will you do that?"

"My da will be back. He'll give it to you. I know he will."

A louder sound in the distance. Was the house going under?

Anna looked up, thinking, frowning. "I will give you the coin," she said, "but you will pay for it another way."

"What do you want?" My lips felt strange as I said it.

"Work for me. Help me gather my weeds and dry them."

I took another step back, suddenly shivering, holding my hands under my shawl, wanting to run, wanting to go to my own house and be safe. Go to Anna's house? Help Anna? I could hardly breathe. "I will," I managed to say.

She pointed to the roof with her cane. While she watched I used the stool to climb. I reached into the thatch, feeling the thick straw dig into my skin and under one of my nails. And there was the coin.

I flew up the road, holding it so hard it made ridges in my palm.

A knot of people were gathered in front. Francey Mallon, my sister Maggie's beau, was sitting on a stone wall, his face dark with anger, staring at Devlin the agent. And the house: only stone walls standing, dust still rising from where the thatched roof had been. Cat and her mother were gone.

I pulled my shawl closer. "Where are they?" I asked a woman who was peering inside. I stood on tiptoes in back of her. The beam of the house had splintered as it fell. It lay in two great pieces on the floor. A rush potato basket lay on its side, empty.

"Can I take the basket, sir?" the woman asked the bailiff.

"Where are they?" I pulled at her sleeve, pulled hard.

She slapped at my hand. "The basket, sir?" she called again.

"The Neelys," I said, holding on to her sleeve.

"Gone." She motioned over her shoulder with her thumb. "Debtors' prison, maybe. They owed rent, owed it for a long time. Someone said they'll be sent to Australia."

I looked at her, horrified. "But that's where criminals go."

"I don't know," she said, her eye still on the basket. She turned away from me, half ducking inside to pick it up.

Gone. *Poor Cat. Poor Mrs. Neely.*

I loosened my clenched hand and looked down. Anna's coin could go back into her thatch. I wouldn't have to go to her house. I wouldn't have to learn her secrets. Her magic. I wouldn't have to see the *sídhe* under her table.

Just under my feet was something of Cat's, a small piece of yarn she had worn in her hair. I reached down to pick it up. *Australia,* I thought.

I circled the house, passing the Neelys' dog, a great black-and-white sheepdog without a name. She lay in front of the tree, tied to the trunk with a piece of rope. When she saw me she lifted herself to her feet, her tail beginning to wag. I could see how thin she was, how easily you could count her ribs. Did she know she had been left there, that Cat and her mother would never come back for her?

I swallowed, watching her sink down again when she realized I hadn't come to let her loose. Her eyes drooped as she rested her head on her paws. I tried not to think of what would happen to her.

Then suddenly someone shouted. "You!"

I looked back over my shoulder at the bailiff's angry face. And I was more frightened than I had been of Anna Donnelly.

I began to run and didn't stop until I reached the cliff road. Then, more slowly, I climbed until I reached the top and sank down to lean my head against the cool rocks of St. Patrick's Well.

A footstep in back of me. The bailiff?

I jerked and opened my hand. The coin slid into the well and Cat's bit of yarn after it. For a moment I could see the glint of the coin, and then it was gone, down, down into water so deep no one would ever find it. The yarn floated on top for a little longer before the water covered that, too.

I turned. The Neelys' dog stood there, the rope still around her neck, the frayed end trailing on the ground. My arms went around her as I sank down to unknot the rope. I rested my head on her matted fur, thinking. The bailiff hadn't called me. He wanted the woman next to me and the basket.

I had lost the coin. The precious coin.

Gone forever.

*And I would have to go to Anna's.*

The dog's back was warm and her ears soft against my fingers. She whined a little and began to lick my face.

At last I stood up. The dog wagged her tail just the least bit. I sighed. "Come, *madra*," I said. "We'll go home."

# Chapter 3

My middle sister, Celia, sat on the wall of the yard, knitting a shawl. I closed my eyes for a moment, thinking of the one I was knitting. It had a hole I could stick my thumb through, and bits of thistle somehow poked through the stitches. A great mess. And Celia had lost no time in telling me so.

She looked up, her eyes widening when she saw the dog. "Where is your head?" She shook her needles furiously.

Fourteen, only two years older than I, and she wanted to be my mother.

"Look at the size of that beast," she said, twitching her little nose like Mallons' goat. "He'd eat as much as I do."

"She. Her name . . . is Maeve." I walked around Celia and inside, blinking in the dim light and nodding at Granda.

Muc the pig in her corner pen snorted when she spotted the dog, and Patch dived into the straw of his bed.

"She won't hurt you, Patcheen." My voice was aimed at the doorway. "She'll be after Celia."

"Really?" Patch said. He raised his head.

"Not really. She's a grand dog. I've named

her after Queen Maeve." I looked down at her. Her muzzle was white, with small black dots where her whiskers grew, almost like the freckles on Maggie's cheeks.

Where was Maggie?

"Grand?" Celia came in with the knitting spilling to her knees. "How do you think we'll manage with another mouth to feed?"

"We just won't feed you, my girl," I said. Big Maggie would have laughed, but my heart wasn't in the teasing. All I could think of was Cat, gone forever, and the coin, and Anna.

"If she sees the potato basket," Celia said, "that *diabhal* will eat them in a gulp."

"She might take your leg as well," I told her. "But she'd be poisoned straightaway."

Granda coughed, his hands over his mouth. I knew he wanted to laugh too, but he wouldn't look at me. He didn't want to tell me what I knew. We could never feed the dog.

"Wait till Maggie sees . . . ," Celia began.

"Where is Maggie?" I asked.

Celia frowned. "Out and down the road with Francey. He came not two minutes ago and wanted to tell her something."

I nodded. About the Neelys, I was sure. I thought about feeding their poor dog.

"Where is the fishing net?" I looked at the

rafters. "The one for fresh water."

Celia shoved the knitting into a basket. Her voice was softer now. "Not Lord Cunningham's stream, is it? You'll find enough trouble without poaching there."

"Poaching?" Granda raised his hand to rake his fingers through his white hair. "That is our land, Irish land. Our stream and our fish. Cunningham, a man who comes once a year, has it all by the terrible might of the English." He turned back to the fire, muttering. "We are paying rent on land that truly belongs to us."

I put my hand on his shoulder and patted his thin back. Then I reached for the net that was looped around a hook. "I won't get caught. Sean Red will be there too," I said. "He always is." I flicked my finger at Celia. "I will feed the dog without taking anything away from the rest of you."

I waved to them from the door, watching Celia's face change as she looked at Maeve. "She's a lovely dog." Her voice floated after me. "Oh, Nory, I will help feed her."

I leaned back in and twitched my nose for a little *Thank you,* then crossed the yard and climbed over the rocky wall. Next to me, Maeve scaled it easily.

"We're going to Cunningham's stream," I told her, feeling a jump in my throat, picturing Cunningham's face, red and mottled from too much mutton. He'd send Devlin his agent to put us out of our house in a breath if he wished, just the way he had the Neelys.

Once I had been hiding, crouched down in the reeds along the stream. I had watched Lord Cunningham talking to Devlin as he fished. He waved his hand at the fields and the cliffs above. "I'd like to get rid of all of them. Filthy hovels, filthy people. I would tear down the houses and let sheep roam among the rocks."

I had wondered where the filthy hovels were. I had wondered about the filthy people. And then I knew. I was one of the filthy people who lived in a filthy hovel. I thought about our house. It was warm and cozy. When the door was closed, the fire lighted the pictures Maggie had drawn on the walls and made wonderful shapes that reached up and up, following the smoke out of the roof, finding their way up to the cliffs.

I saw Cunningham's big house now, with its huge stone wall, and farther down was Devlin's. Even that was larger than any in Maidin Bay.

"Not a sound." I put my hand on the dog's soft head.

Small bushes hung on to the sides of the stream in front of us. It was a ribbon of water, dotted with rocks like black turtles raising their backs to the sun.

Sean Red was there somewhere, waiting to surprise the fish. Even I wouldn't be able to spot him unless I caught a glimpse of the flame of his hair.

I slid down the bank and landed in the mud at the edge. Lord Cunningham was probably at his dinner, thinking of the fish that had been cooked for him instead of the ones Sean and I would take.

And then Sean was next to me, pointing along the rocks under the water where he had strung his net. I tucked up my petticoat and waded into the icy water.

"Don't splash," he said as I wound my net a few feet away from his.

"Don't you splash." I flicked a few drops at him.

He laughed. He was never cold and I was always shivering.

"Where did you get him?" Sean asked, thumb pointing at Maeve.

"Her?" I bit my lip. "I found her."

Sean was satisfied. I would have been asking question after question, but he was looking down into the stream, waiting for his fish.

We stood there for a long time. My toes were numb and my ankles. Sean stood stone-still, almost carved into the river, waiting.

A small, silvery school of fish came, veering away from Sean's net, around the rocks, and caught by mine. We slapped at them, tossing them up on the bank. I was soaking wet, freezing. My face burned, my eyes teared. Maeve dashed after the flapping fish.

The water swirled as a larger fish broke the surface, chasing the school of fish ahead of it. Now it was caught. It swam along the net, trying to escape.

We dived for it together. I flung myself across the rocks on top of it, Sean yelling, both of us breathless. "A beauty," I said.

"It's huge," Sean said.

Then suddenly a man on a horse splashed down the shallow thread of water toward us. Lord Cunningham! He shouted as he rode, the tails at his coat flapping against his boots, his riding crop in his hand.

I tried to scramble up, but my petticoat was heavy with mud and water, and the rocks were slippery under my bare feet.

Sean held the big fish under one arm. At the same time he put his hand on my back, trying to push me up the bank.

At last I heaved myself over the top and reached back to help him. But Cunningham leaned over the side of the horse. "Give that fish back," he shouted, his face red. He lashed out with the crop, catching Sean on the shoulder, tearing his shirt.

Still Sean tried to hold the fish, tried to crawl out of the horse's way. *"Rith leat,"* he called to me. "Run."

Above the horse's hooves we heard a deep growl. Maeve, teeth bared, tore into the water.

In that instant I saw the bailiff coming, saw us out of our house. I saw Celia's face.

"Stay, Maeve," I called to her, terrified. "Stay."

The dog stopped, that good dog, stood as still in the water as Sean had done. Then a miracle! Something else caught Cunningham's attention. A man on a horse was riding toward the big house. We scrambled away as Cunningham turned his horse and splashed through the water, riding back the way he had come.

Maeve shook the water off herself, panting, and nosed into my hand. "A fish for you, two fish," I said when I caught my breath. I looked at Sean. "Do you think Cunningham knew who we were?"

"He mixes all of us together." Sean

rubbed his shoulder. "We're safe, I think."

"One thing," I said slowly. "He will not forget Maeve."

# Chapter 4

I pushed open the door of our house, my share of the catch held up in my skirt. But as soon as I ducked inside, I knew something was wrong. Maggie stood at the hearth, the glow from the peat fire lighting the tears in her eyes. Granda sat on the three-legged stool, his head in his hands. And Patch was burrowed under the straw of his bed, his scrap of blanket tucked under his chin. Even Biddy, our hen, and her two sisters were clucking as they dashed back and forth on the earthen floor.

Celia didn't look at me. She banged down the potato pot, then rooted through the basket in the corner, tossing out an old coat of Granda's and Da's boot without a sole.

"What is it?" I said. "Tell me."

Maggie came toward me. "I'm going." Her mouth was unsteady. "Leaving for America."

I raised my hands, the fish sliding out of my skirt and onto the floor.

"Going across the sea," said Granda, biting his lip.

*Brooklyn, New York. Milk in cans. Maggie without us.*

Maggie reached out with her big arms and held me so tight I could hardly breathe. "It's the Neelys," she said.

"Out of their house," I said. And then I knew: the anger on Francey's face, his eyes flashing. He had seen it all.

"He will not stay," Maggie said. "Not one more month. Not in this land with the English so cruel."

"But that's not the way it's supposed to be," I said. "We are all to go. Someday. A long time from now."

Maggie shook her head. "There's never enough to eat. When I'm gone there will be that little bit extra."

I hardly listened. "We'll go when Patch is grown, when there's money."

"Francey has enough money for the passage." Maggie held on to my shoulders. "We need our own place, our own family. We want it to be in Brooklyn, America. Free."

Just then Celia crashed the potato pot into the wall. "Ah, here, underneath." She held up the comb. It was missing four teeth, but the tiny pink stones along the top glowed whenever I held it up to the sun.

"I will take it with me when I go," Celia said.

"It's my comb," I said. "From Mam."

"Go where?" Maggie asked.

Granda and Patch stared at Celia.

"I am going to America myself. Straight-away." She began to run the comb through her hair.

"My comb," I said. "Da said it was mine."

Celia held it high over her head. I jumped for it, and between us, the comb snapped in two. I looked at the piece in my hand, shocked. Mam's comb.

"How are you going to America?" Granda asked Celia.

"I will get the money for passage somehow," Celia said. "I will walk to Galway."

"You can't even manage the walk to Ballilee." I held my piece of the comb tightly in my hand. "Who'll take care of Patch?" A poor wee mess he was with a sore on his mouth and a scratch on his cheek from chasing Biddy the hen. "Who will watch him?"

"He loves you best, Nory," Maggie whispered.

Celia looked at Patch in the bed, then closed her eyes. After a moment she said, "I will take care of him. I have decided. I will go to America when Da gets home."

*Who will take care of me?* I rushed outside, sliding over the fish on the floor.

Maggie called after me but I heard

Granda say, "Let her go."

*Go where?* I asked myself.

Head down, I walked along the Mallons' path. Sean's brother Long Liam was lugging rocks around the side of the house. They were piled as high as his waist. "I will build a shed for meself," Liam had told me. "I'll put me feet on one wall at night and me head on the other without having to curl over like a snail in the house with three brothers."

I didn't want him to see me with my red face and teary eyes so I kept walking, the mud coming up between my toes. I climbed the stile to the cemetery and started across. First was St. Erna's shrine. The statue was old and chipped so Da had built a stone roof over the saint's head and a wall around his back. "It'll keep the old monk out of the rain for another hundred years or so," he had said.

Next I stopped at Mam's grave and said a quick "May the angels lead thee into Paradise." I remembered Mam tossing hay in our field with Da one fall day. Dust and bits of straw had swirled around us, and Mam had asked what we'd like to name the baby that was coming.

I had looked up at the well. "If it's a boy, it should be Patrick."

Mam clapped her hands. "That's what we'll do, Nory."

I had danced around the field with Da, singing, "We'll call him Patch."

And now Mam was under the grass and Maggie would be off to America. What would Da say when he came up the road from Galway and Maggie wasn't at the top of the hill waiting for him?

I saw Sean coming, looking for me. He must have heard the news. I stood up quickly, wiping my eyes, and in my hurry ripped my toenail on a stone. I sank down again and rocked back and forth, holding my toe. And by then, Sean was there, sitting next to me, neither of us saying a word, until I dusted myself off. "It's time to go back," I said.

I looked toward Anna Donnelly's house. I'd have to go there, but not until after the wedding. I promised myself that. And something else. I told myself I'd never let Maggie know how terrible I felt. I could do that, couldn't I? Sing and pretend to be happy until she took the road to Galway.

Could I?

# Chapter 5

And so I didn't cry, not when I saw the bag Maggie had made to take with her, and not when I hung our good dresses outside to air on a rope. I tried to listen as Maggie taught me how to smoor the night fire. *"Here, Nory, see. The fire has never gone out. Not once in a hundred years. Cover it over with ash, but leave one piece of turf burning so you can blow it into life in the morning."*

Then, at last, it was Maggie's wedding day. We opened the door early to see the sun and the good luck it would bring. It was there coming up over the hill, even though ragged bits of mist still hovered over the fields, and the cliffs were hidden under a cover of gray.

Father Harte said the blessing, and afterward, Paddy Mulligan's bow flew over the fiddle strings as Long Liam's fingers pounded the skin of his drum.

That night flames shot up from the bonfire in front of the house, and Maggie danced with Francey, danced in Mam's red dress, her hair streaming out in back of her. We clapped for them, all of us, the Mallons, the cousins who had come from Ballilee,

34

and even Anna Donnelly, leaning against the wall, her pipe in her mouth. I sang until my voice was hoarse, and in between, Sean Red pulled me up to dance around the doorstep with my green dress, the wrinkles mostly out now, swirling around me.

"You look like Queen Maeve herself," Sean said, smiling at me.

When the hills in back of us began to brighten, Francey took up one of my hands and Maggie the other. We circled the house to the music and had one last dance together, Granda and Celia, and Patch half asleep, all of us laughing and crying as we held each other.

It seemed we'd hardly slept when it was day, the day I dreaded. They'd leave this morning to walk the road to Galway to board the *Emma Pearl*. They'd never come back to Maidin Bay. A long road, it was. Da had told us it wound around the coast like a ball of yarn let loose, but if you stayed on it, you'd reach the port and the ships.

I turned now and the straw of my bed crackled beneath me. Maggie stood in the open door. As quietly as I could, I crawled over Patch, and then Celia, and rolled out of the bed. I wanted to say goodbye to Maggie by myself.

Outside, Francey slept against the wall

with his brothers, and Paddy the fiddler was snoring with his head on his case.

"Shhh." Maggie motioned to me to follow, and when I caught up, pulled me along the cliff road. "It's my last chance to talk to you," she said.

A pair of gannets flew high over us, going toward the sea.

"I'll miss them," Maggie said. "I'll miss you."

My voice didn't sound like my own. "I will be in Brooklyn, New York, myself, one day with you."

Maggie turned to me. I could see the flecks of gray in her blue eyes and count every one of her freckles, we were that close. "You are the heart of this family," she said, "with your songs."

I shook my head a little. I couldn't speak.

"You will take care of Patcheen and the others." She stopped.

It was hard to swallow. "Celia is older."

She smiled. "Celia is loyal and true, and between the two of you, you'll see, Da will find his home and warm hearth the way he left them."

At the top of the cliff a thin mist came from Patrick's Well; beyond that the sea was a shimmer of silver. "Da's out there," I said.

Maggie nodded, her eyes wet. "When you

see him, tell him we'll be together again someday." She took a piece of my hair between her fingers. "I want to tell you, you who are always in a hurry . . ."

"I don't see the currachs out on the water today," I said, to make her think of something else.

"Everyone is sleeping after the wedding. They're too tired to fish." She gave my hair a bit of a pull. "Think of me when you're not sure of something, Nory." Her face was serious, her big eyes holding me. "Know that I'll be there on the other side of the water. Think of what I'd say, what I'd do."

If only I could tell her about the coin and Anna Donnelly. But what would she say? What would she think?

Maggie touched my face. "I don't even know why I tell you that. You will know what to do yourself. You are a great girl, *a stór*."

A great girl. I loved the sound of it. And then we heard the trill of music. "Paddy Mulligan with his fiddle out again," I said.

"He's playing for Granda," Maggie said, "for Granda's war."

"The War of 1798," I said.

We stood there thinking about the story we had heard so many times, Granda with his friends, young and fighting with the French, hoping we'd be like the Americans and have our freedom from the English. "They had a new country out there in the States," Granda always said. "They had freed themselves of the English just twenty years earlier. Why not us? Why not?"

I hummed an old war song about the Irish and their courage, and Maggie finished with me.

But all their courage hadn't been enough. The English had an army, and souls of vinegar, and they had killed and killed, and we were still not free.

Maggie and I went back together, and Patch ran to tell us Francey had gone to the Mallon house for his things. Maggie rolled up Mam's wedding dress and tucked it back in the straw basket. "For you both someday," she told Celia and me.

I raised my head. "We will bring it when we come to Brooklyn."

Celia nodded, her little nose as pink as Mallons' goat, her eyes swollen.

Maggie was ready to go. The Mallons, all of them, waited outside. For a long moment Maggie hugged us, Granda and Celia, Patch and me. Granda put the sign of the cross on her forehead with his thumb. He reached into his pocket and pulled out a small piece of blue cloth. "Inside," he said, "is a wee bit of salt. Take it against the *sidhe*."

"Oh, Granda." She rubbed the bag between her palms. "I will keep it always to remember you."

We walked with them, even old Granny Mallon tottering along. We passed the church so Father Harte could say a last prayer. Then we started up the hill. Paddy played the fiddle and Sean said, "Sing, Nory."

At first I couldn't open my mouth, but I thought of what Maggie had said on our walk together. I lifted my chin and began a wedding song, the sweet sound of it filling my head.

At the crossroads, Francey lifted his pack higher, and Maggie turned to walk backward. "We will be together again," she called. "Hold on to that."

We waved until she stumbled and Francey took her hand. For another moment we could see them; then they were gone. Patch sank to the ground, crying, "I want my own Maggie."

I wanted to sink down too. Instead I brushed my hands across my hair. *Great girl, a stór.* I bent over, holding Patch the way Maggie would have, rocking him. "You are a great lad, *a stór,*" I said, and began to cry with him.

# Chapter 6

Today the sky was blue and the plants high. I was tired of knitting with only the light from the hearth to guide my stitches. I was tired of that one room with its earthen floor tramped down by Ryan feet over the last hundred years. The floor was so uneven that only the three-legged stool was steady on it. And our heels had worn small round bowls into it large enough to hold puddles of mussels before St. Patrick's Day, and limpets after that.

*Fuafar* limpets. I hated the slimy taste of them.

The room seemed so empty without Maggie. I closed my eyes, remembering when Granda taught me my first song: "Wee Falorie Man." The room was filled with all of us: Granda and Da, Mam and Maggie, Celia and me. I sang it through, *"Rumpty tumpty toddy man,"* as Granda thumped his blackthorn stick against the floor and everyone laughed.

"What are you thinking about?" Celia asked.

"Mam," I said. "And Maggie."

"Don't," she whispered, holding up her hand.

I took a quick look at Patch. Every time one of us said Maggie's name, he cried.

"I would go down to the sea today and gather some kelp," I said, "if only I had someone to come with me."

Granda nodded. "It's a good day for it."

Patch grabbed my sleeve. "I will go to the sea with you, Nory."

"I knew that, didn't I?" Celia and I glanced at each other over his head, smiling at him. I tucked up his hem so he could walk easily.

"Someday I will have a suit of clothes," he said as I turned him around.

"Not yet, *a stór*," I whispered. "We won't let the *sídhe* know we have a boy instead of a girl."

"I know. They'd rather steal boys." He nodded at me uneasily. "I'm not afraid."

"No," I said. "And you will be the greatest help today." I patted his cheek, then looped the basket over my arm.

We took the path that led down to the beach and back up. A narrow loop it was, full of grass with spikes that rustled as the wind blew, trying to keep us away from the sea.

We went on down the path with Patch pulling on my hand, veering this way and that to pick up stones for his collection.

41

They all looked the same to me, but he'd stare at one and throw it away, nod at another and stick it in his pocket.

"Nice, Patcheen," I said as he held up a blue one. "It's like your eyes, blue stone eyes."

He thought about it. "Yes," he said, and ran ahead of me onto the sand, ready to chase the seabirds and watch the currachs bobbing beyond the surf. Long Liam and Michael Mallon were out in one of them, fishing.

I shaded my eyes. Was Maggie across the sea yet? *"Number 416 on Smith Street,"* I sang to myself, *"Maggie, and Francey, and Mary Mallon together in Brooklyn, New York."* Maggie had said it over and over so I'd never forget.

I looked up at the cliffs. A slash of stone, whiter than the rest, pointed the way home for the men in the currachs. "When I see that stone," Long Liam always said, "I know it's only a bit of surf between me and the warmth of our hearth."

Were there cliffs like ours above the houses on Smith Street? I had asked Maggie and Francey about it, but they had shrugged their shoulders, smiling.

Sean came toward me. He passed the spot where the cliffs hung over him in a dark and fearful arch and made the sign of the cross over himself. Up there, years ago, men let themselves down on ropes to narrow ledges. They'd catch the seabirds for their meat and gather eggs from their nests. One of them had been called Tague, Francey had told me. Tague had the courage of Queen Maeve, but without thinking he had reached out in the wind one day, and fallen . . . fallen.

I shivered, but then Sean was next to me. "The tide is still out," he said. "Not a bit of kelp coming in."

I wasn't disappointed. The tide would soon turn. And if we had luck the water would drag back enough of the weed to fill our baskets for soup, with a little left to sweeten the potatoes.

I looked up at him. "I miss Maggie," I said. "There's such a space in our family, a space at our hearth. Do you —"

He held up his hand. He knew I was going to ask about Francey. I should have known he wouldn't answer. If something could be said in two words, he'd say it in one. But this time I was wrong. "I think of America all the time," he said. "I think of my sister, Mary, and my brother Francey." His jaw was clenched. "If it takes me forever, I will be there too." He touched my cheek, a feather

43

of a touch. "And you with me as well."

We stood there looking at each other until I remembered Patch. I turned quickly. "Patcheen. You are too close to the edge of the water!"

He raced along the sand, arms out, head up, looking beautiful with his fine light hair.

I felt a quick pain in my chest, imagining the *sidhe* sneaking up from their fairy ring and dragging the boy children down. I chased Patch the way he chased the birds and we fell over each other, tumbling and laughing, with Sean Red in back of us, pointing as the tide began to turn. The green kelp spilled toward us in the curl of the waves.

It was then I heard Celia. She stood at the edge of the path, her skirt blowing, motioning to me. I left my basket and ran, but by the time I reached the spot she was gone. Granda? Was he sick? What had happened?

"Patch," I called. "We're going home."

"Without the kelp?" Then he saw my face and took my hand.

We hurried home to see a brown horse tethered at the end of our path, and our door half open.

*Devlin the agent*, I thought. My mouth was suddenly dry. Had Lord Cunningham sent him here? Was it about stealing the fish?

And Maeve? I wanted to go back to the strand to hide. But Celia and Granda were alone in there with him. I edged into the doorway to stand against the wall, still holding Patch's hand.

Devlin sat at the hearth on the three-legged stool. Granda and Celia stood together in the middle of the floor. I could see Celia's hands trembling just a bit.

Devlin looked up as he saw me. "I've been telling the others," he said, "that I have been to the Mallons'."

Mallons'? What was he talking about? I looped my shawl over the peg.

"They have done well for themselves this year." Devlin picked at something in his mustache. "They have built a shed. Improved the property. I have been there to raise their rent."

Anger burned in my chest, and I could feel it in Granda and Celia. I thought of Liam's work. The heavy rocks, the hours. I closed my teeth tight over the edge of my tongue.

Devlin stared at the fire. "The rent will be due soon."

"Not until December." I could feel Patch shrinking behind me.

"Our da is working for the rent, fishing out of Galway," Celia said.

45

Devlin rocked back on the stool. "There is talk of trouble in the fields."

"What fields?" Granda asked, his voice stronger than I had heard it in a long time. "What trouble?"

Devlin spread his hands. "The potatoes are black. In Sligo."

"A long way away," Granda said, but I could see the fear in his eyes. I knew what he was thinking; it was the story of the potatoes failing when Da was a boy. Everything else had gone to pay the rent, and there was no food. People had starved, even one of Da's brothers.

A thump of fear in my chest. Could it happen to us?

"Sligo is not so far after all," Devlin said, and stood up. "Potatoes or no potatoes, there will be rent to pay. Without the rent, the tenants will go, and the houses will be tumbled. The sheep will come in and graze on the empty fields. I have come to warn you."

I could hear Granda's breathing and see Celia clutch at her knitting. But before any of us could think of what to say, he was gone.

# Chapter 7

It had been a strange fall, lovely in the mornings, with heavy rain and fingers of clouds reaching down from the cliffs every afternoon. And today was the same. I thought about Anna; I knew I had to go to her. If only I could stay near our fire, picturing horses clopping down Smith Street, Brooklyn, in the orange flames, imagining Maggie home with us.

I left the house with Maeve a step in back of me and walked along the edge of the field. The potatoes grew strong, the leaves large and flat. I pictured roots swelling under the ground, the tubers round by now. My mouth watered. I had a headache because I had given half my breakfast to Maeve. Celia had given half hers, too. I had seen her.

I lifted my head. There was something in the air. A strange smell. I tried to think of what it was, but the wind blew across the field, tangling my hair and pulling at my petticoat. By the time I straightened myself out, the smell had drifted away.

At the stone wall I searched out the sea in the distance. It shimmered in the sunlight, but underfoot my toes squished in the mud, and next to me, Maeve's fur was matted with it.

Maeve saw something that I didn't see. A movement in the distance? Something wild? She was off in an instant, ears back, loping across the field.

Da would have loved her. Da with his blue eyes and his laugh like Maggie's. Da on a ship, sails billowing.

I passed Sean Red's cottage. A brown wren worked on a nest in the roof's thatching. Inside, Sean's mother scolded someone in her rough voice. Just past was the path to Anna Donnelly's.

The crows *chew-chew*ed overhead, but everything else was still. Across the field Anna's cow lowed, wanting to be milked. I looked for the pail and went across to her. Kneeling with my head on her side, squirting the milk into the pail, I thought how warm and sweet it would be on my tongue. I wished I could hurry home with it, pail and all, bending a little, the wire handles making ridges in my fingers.

I could see all of us in a circle. In the center, the pot of potatoes, small mountains in a sea of white milk.

We hadn't had milk since last year when Da first came home, and there'd be none this year until he returned.

"Did I ask you to milk my own cow?" a voice asked.

Anna stood at her doorway.

I gave the cow a pat and a push and reached for the pail. I answered her in the same harsh way. "Your cow needed milking."

"Your tongue is sharp enough to cut a stone," she said.

I wanted to say that no one's tongue was as sharp as hers. I never would, though. I raised my head. It almost seemed as if her eyes were twinkling. But then her hand went to her mouth.

I turned to see what she was seeing, and it was Maeve, flying across the field. "My dog," I said.

"A *madra*," she said. As small as she was, Anna bent toward the dog, waiting. Maeve passed me and stopped at Anna's feet. They stood together, faces close. Anna reached out to touch Maeve's ears, her back, her sides, the dog nuzzling her shoulder.

"My son had a dog like this once," Anna said.

I couldn't imagine Anna with a son or a dog.

"Maeve was Cat Neely's dog," I said slowly.

"And they are gone," she said. "And my coin as well."

I opened my mouth to tell her what had happened. But a sound came from the distance. Someone in the valley had wailed. Someone with a high thin voice.

I swiveled around, the milk sloshing over the edge of the pail. "What was that?" The cow moved uneasily.

Anna raised her head, her sharp chin jutting out. She leaned against her cane with one hand, but the other hand, stained with peat, was up against the cottage doorway, trembling the slightest bit.

Anna hobbled out, going around to the small field of potatoes that wandered up the hill in back. "I can smell it," she said. "I've smelled it before. Years ago."

I followed her, stopping to slide the pail of milk into the doorway. The smell was stronger now, coming in waves on the wind. And then I knew.

The potatoes.

"Yes. Something poisoning the potatoes," Anna said as if she knew what I was thinking.

"Not yours," I told her, looking over the field. I stood on tiptoes to see the edge of our own field, the potato plants as strong and the stems as thick as they had been when I passed them earlier. "And not ours."

She bent over the potatoes, hobbling from

50

one plant to another, patting the leaves, touching the stems. She turned and pointed to the spade that leaned against the wall. "Bring the loy."

I hurried back across the field, stepping around Anna's pig.

I gripped the spade hard. *Think about green leaves*, I told myself. *Think about the sun in the sky and Da fishing on a big ship. Think about good things.*

*What else?*

*A red wedding dress. Number 416 Smith Street in Brooklyn.*

*Think about...*

*Stories of famine, people dying in their houses. Da's little brother. A boy like Patch.*

*Please let the potatoes be all right.*

I dug where Anna pointed, Maeve in the way, ears lifting gently in the wind. I eased the spade under the firm leaves of a potato plant, watching the earth come away in thick clods. The plant tilted, and I edged the spade out again.

Anna leaned over me, leaned so close that I could smell ... what was it? A lovely smell. The smell of spring, or fuchsia growing along the walls in August. She reached out to pull the plant up, to touch the small clump of potatoes, brown and firm, to brush away the soil with her wrinkled hands.

51

"They're all right." I let out my breath and uncurled my fingers. I could feel the sun on my head.

Anna's eyes gleamed. "Fine potatoes." The lines around her mouth softened. She almost smiled.

"Fine." I began to smile back, but I felt a sudden pain in my chest: *The coin hidden under the water of St. Patrick's Well. How much food would it have bought? A coin that hadn't even had a wish to it.*

Anna shook more soil off the potatoes and her face hardened again. "Not even enough for a meal. A wee meal with almost no milk." She talked to herself as she walked past me to her door. "It is still a way to the harvest."

I stood there, tracing circles in the soil with my toes, watching Maeve follow her inside. Then I went after them slowly, not daring to put my foot on the step. "The dog," I called.

From inside there was silence.

"It's not that I want her to come with me," I said.

Anna was back at the door.

"We can't feed her," I told her. "There's not even enough for all of us now."

She brought her pipe to her mouth.

"Would you . . . ," I began.

"I would," she said.

The wail came again. I shaded my eyes and looked across the valley to see the cliffs in the distance and the tree that sheltered Patrick's Well. Where was that sound coming from?

Anna sighed. "Go back to your own potatoes, this day," she said. "Go and look carefully. Look for the black."

I nodded. The smell was stronger now, that terrible smell. "I will come again tomorrow," I said.

"To spill more of my milk."

I looked back over my shoulder. She and Maeve stood together. Maeve had decided where she belonged. She didn't even try to follow me as I crossed the field. When I glanced back, she was looking up at Anna, tail waving like a plume of wheat in the wind. Anna had her hand lightly on the dog's head, but I could see her face. I could see she was afraid.

I stood there for another moment; then I started for home.

# Chapter 8

The sun was high now, the dew gone. The stubble of weeds was prickly under my feet. I took the shortcut across Mallons' field.

Sean Red and the rest of the Mallon family were outside, almost all. Liam was gone, probably fishing at the edge of the bay, but the others were in the back field. Even Granny Mallon in an old woolen nightgown torn up the side was propped up against the stone wall. Mrs. Mallon, her hands on her thick hips, looked grim; she didn't answer when I called, "Bless all here."

Sean raised his hand. "Someone is screaming in the next valley."

I crossed my arms over my chest, beginning to shiver.

"She's being taken by a *sídhe*." He was trying to smile. "Pulled down under the earth."

"Don't say that."

"Do you think someone is screaming because of the potatoes?" he asked.

I opened my mouth to tell him about Anna but Mrs. Mallon was moving quickly down the field, her red skirt pulled up around her large legs. She knelt over one of

54

the beds, groaning, digging at one of the plants with her hands. I followed Sean and his brother Michael to see what she was looking at. It hardly seemed like much. It was just the tiniest edge of the leaf that had shriveled and curled under, but it was enough to see that the stem underneath was soft and pulpy.

"Look across," Mrs. Mallon said in her harsh voice. "There." She pointed with one thick finger. "And there."

It was everywhere. A leaf lying back against a stem as if it had no strength to stand up by itself. Another stem seemed to lose color in front of our eyes. I backed away, stepping on one plant, shaking the edge of my skirt where the plant had left a smear of brownish ooze. I tried not to take a deep breath because the smell was stronger now.

I took another step, seeing Granny Mallon, her pipe in one hand. "Without potatoes we will starve to death," she said, beginning to rock back and forth.

"I have to go home," I said.

But no one listened. The Mallons were walking across the beds, and Mrs. Mallon began to cry with a hard, deep sound.

"I'm sorry for your trouble." I bit my lip. I didn't know why I said it. It was something Da and Maggie whispered at wakes, when someone had died. I picked up my skirt and ran toward home.

My breath came in ragged gulps as I climbed over the stile, looking at our own potato plants. They were too close to the Mallons' field. If it had been the *sidhe* with their long fingers, they could have reached across the fields and touched and turned everything black.

I stopped to look at one plant, and then another. Green. Firm. Lovely.

Safe?

"Granda," I called as soon as I saw our roof and the smoke drifting away from it. "Celia." I ran down the path, ducking my head, as I burst in through the open doorway.

"Granda."

It was dark inside the cottage, the fire low. Celia sat at the hearth, knitting, her eyes closed, counting the pattern in her mind.

"It's the potatoes," I said.

"Anna's?"

"No. At least not yet." I shook my head. "It's Mallons' field."

Granda pulled himself to his feet. "Then ours." He limped to the doorway, pulling the spade off the hook on the wall.

Celia and I followed him outside, Patch's hand in mine. We walked along between the beds just as the Mallons had done. The spade dug into the earth. We held our breath as Granda lifted up the small potatoes, then patted them under the earth again.

He rubbed his hands against his sides and smiled as he saw us staring at him. But his smile was a terrible one, and his eyes were wild.

Celia walked ahead of us. Inside, she reached into the bin for potatoes. She had to scrape the bottom for them. The last of the old harvest was on us.

I looked at Granda again. He was terrified and trying not to tell us.

"We can gather limpets," I said, "and mussels on the rocks."

He smiled a little. "Aye."

"And Sean and I caught that wonderful fish. We could catch another."

"Grand."

"And we could buy bread." She held up her knitting. "I will walk to Ballilee and sell my shawl. It is almost finished." She stared at me.

"Lovely," I said a little grudgingly. My shawl was hanging in its bag on the hook. A shawl with a hole. A splotch of mud. Knots as thick as the wild onions along the river.

"I will finish my own straightaway," I told

her. "And make mittens from the last of the wool."

"Yes, fine," Celia said, but I knew she didn't believe it.

I didn't believe it either. Much less a pair of mittens. I had never once been able to do the thumb.

"But remember." Celia leaned forward. "Our potatoes are still healthy. Not a mark. Not a spot."

We all nodded, looking out the open doorway. She was right. The potatoes were still fine.

# Chapter 9

I was dreaming, rocked in the currach on Maidin Bay, small fingerlets of waves underneath me. There was a pull on Sean Red's hook. Drops of water ran off the line as it came in, the fish a flash of silver under the surface.

But what was that smell? I opened my eyes. It had been my turn for the hearth side, so there was no need to climb over Celia and Patch. I rolled out of the bed, the straw crackling under me. The glow from the hearth was just bright enough for me to see Granda huddled in the bed on the other side of the room.

I stood there to be sure they were still asleep. But how could they sleep with the smell that was drifting in under the door?

Three steps, then I eased the door open. Outside it was bright as day. The moon was up, full and white, throwing sharp shadows away from me. I heard thunder somewhere, though, and the air was damp and heavy.

Nighttime belonged to the *sidhe*, so I was afraid to take more than a few steps, but it was far enough. The potato stalks leaned against each other, limp and wet, the leaves shapeless and dripping.

I pulled up the edge of my petticoat to cover my nose and backed against the wall of the house. My throat felt thick. In my mind was Granny Mallon's voice: *"Without potatoes we will starve to death."*

I couldn't stop shivering. All our food for the next season was gone. The fish we had talked about, the mussels, the limpets. They would not be enough.

I didn't know how long I'd been standing there when I heard Granda come outside with the loy in his hand. I knew it was morning, though. A pale yellow sun appeared and was hidden again.

"Granda," I said, reaching out to touch his sleeve.

"I thought you were sleeping," he said.

I followed him, trying to walk on my toes, trying to keep my petticoat above the ground, out of the ooze of the potatoes.

He began to dig, pulling up a potato that was no bigger than my thumb, and then another.

"Nory," he said, out of breath. "Wake your sister. We will take up what is here. At least we will have something."

I started for the door, stopping halfway. If there were no potatoes, not any, how would we plant the eyes next year? It was hard to walk, almost as if I were at the edge of the surf with the water pounding at me, holding me back. I didn't get to the doorway. Celia was standing there.

She ducked inside for the smaller spade with the broken handle, calling over her shoulder, "It's all right, Patcheen. Go back to sleep."

We ran across the field. I didn't bother now about my skirt or the ooze on my feet. I tied the edge of my shawl over my nose and mouth and began to dig with a small shelf of rock.

A burst of wind came up, driving the smell toward us. Granda's hair blew as he worked, as Celia bent over, gagging.

Now Patch was at the edge of the field, coming toward us.

I shook my head and turned over the earth. A potato, fist sized, enough for a child's breakfast. I turned over another, but I could dig my thumb into its soft spots.

We could cut out the spots, cook the rest. I put it aside. "There, Patcheen," I said. What would happen to him? What would happen to all of us? "We'll make a pile on top of the wall. We'll cook the ones that look the best. And then we'll dig a trench to keep the perfect ones."

I picked up the next small cluster; they

turned to mush in my hands. I threw them away from me, wiping my fingers on my skirt, clamping my lips over my mouth, swallowing hard. My shawl slipped away from my face and I held my arm up across my nose and mouth and breathed in, kept breathing.

I tried not to watch Granda pile up the soil, digging as fast as he could, his shirt soaked, his face filthy. How old he looked!

Celia watched him too. When he saw us, he shook his head. "Let me help while I can," he said.

I wanted to put my arms around him. I wanted to tell him I loved him. I wanted to tell him to lie in his bed with the door closed against that terrible smell.

He'd never do that.

I stared down at the earth. What would we do if something happened to him?

Patch looked at me, but I just handed him tiny potatoes to put along the wall.

By the time we were finished, there was a small hill of them, enough to last for only a few days. At the other end of the field was the trench. Instead of neat piles to be covered with soft earth and dug up for food all winter, there was one thin row of tiny potatoes, maybe enough for a few weeks, not enough for a winter, not even enough for the fall, and surely not enough to save for planting in the spring.

Granda leaned against the wall at the edge of the field, looking up at the cliffs. He had tears in his eyes, tears like Da's the day he left us for the ship, and tears like Maggie's when she set out. Da wouldn't even know what had happened to us, and neither would Maggie.

Patch was in front of me, his thin clothes caked with grime. "We'll go to the stream," I said. "It will be cool and wet and we'll march ourselves in."

"And dry ourselves off in the sun." Celia turned to Granda. "Will you come with us?"

He shook his head slowly. He was bent against the wall, his hands spread out against the rocks.

The stream gurgled as we went across the field, Patch's hand in mine. "A little string of water, isn't it," I said, "that winds down from the cliffs."

"Cunningham's stream," Celia said.

"We are too tired to go to the sea," I said. She nodded.

I began to sing, ". . . *wee melodie man, the rumpty tumpty toddy man . . .*"

Patch looked up at me. "We don't care about the potatoes, do we?"

I wanted to put my hands over my ears. I

didn't want to think about potatoes, or being hungry, or the pain tapping in back of my eyes.

But I tried to follow it through. No potatoes. No food. But Da would bring money back.

*Enough money for food and rent?*

I worried it around in my head, back and forth like a cat chasing a mouse in the field.

Lord Cunningham's house was above us. Still. Silent. I wondered what he thought about all this. Was he glad? Was he thinking of sheep grazing on empty land?

I put one foot into the shallow water. It was icy cold. In a second my toes were numb. I drew in my breath, pulling my foot out.

"That water is too cold for me," Patch said.

"Yes." I dipped my petticoat into the stream, then raised it to his face, cleaning his mouth, his nose, seeing his freckles like Maggie's and his blue eyes like Da's.

I leaned over and sang to him as I rocked him back and forth.

# Chapter 10

We went to our beds early. If we had left the door open, we could have seen the sky, still bright, with the sun just beginning to slide away in back of the cliffs.

We didn't do that, though. We didn't want to see those poor black potatoes taken by the *sidhe*. We didn't want to smell what was left of them.

Instead we lay there with only the gleam from the smoored fire, worrying. Overhead the hens were clucking on their rope. They made me think of Maggie. Long ago she had strung that rope across the eaves for them to roost.

"The thing about hens," she had said, "is that they argue every night, clucking away. They're trying to decide whether they should fly back to Norway where they first came from."

I remembered watching as she said, "Be kind to them so they'll stay one more day and lay another egg or two for us."

And now Celia was saying we'd be wringing their necks for three meals.

I shuddered. "What about the eggs?"

"We will close the door and go to Maggie

in Brooklyn, New York," Celia said. "We will do that straightaway."

*Horses clopping down the street, milk in pails, froth on top.*

"We will ask Sean Red to write us a letter," Celia said, "to tell Maggie we're coming."

I didn't say that Sean knew only letters, not words, and not all of the letters anyway. I cleared my throat. "What money will you use to send the letter?" I asked. "And what to get us on a ship?"

She sighed. "We will wait for Da. Yes, all we have to do is find food for each day. Maybe we could do that."

The hens stopped their clucking. They were going to stay another day with us as well. My eyes wanted to close. "We will have eggs," I said.

Next to me Patch was almost asleep too. "Eggs, eggs, eggs," he whispered, and was still.

"And we will eat just one meal, every night," Celia said. "We can spend our time searching for food."

I went to sleep at last and dreamed of Anna. I couldn't remember what it was, but in the morning I awoke suddenly, my heart pounding and a sharp pain in my stomach. Celia dragged herself up across me and opened the door to let the hens out. I pulled the cover up over my nose. "Close the door quickly," I said. "The smell is. . ." I couldn't even think of a word.

*"Fuafar,"* Celia said.

*Fuafar.* Disgusting. Yes. I had to get up. I had to do something.

"Aha." Celia reached into Biddy's basket. "A nice brown egg for Patch." She smiled at him. "I will cook it for you this minute."

I rolled out of the straw and onto my knees to say my morning prayers. I prayed that I would look out the door and the smell would be gone and the potatoes would be growing strong in the stony field. But I knew that wouldn't happen.

"I will go now to Anna's," I told them as I stood up.

Celia began to cry. "We just have to hold on, all of us," she said through her tears.

I turned back to her and put my arms around her. "We will," I said. "Somehow."

For a moment she cried even harder. Then she patted my cheeks.

I went across the field, pictures of Da in my head, one after another, his blue eyes, the color of the sky over Maidin Bay, his arms strong, angling for a fish from the cliff top. He'd lean forward as he told stories about his first fishing trip, about meeting

Mam with her curls tied back with a piece of string. I wanted him so much I could almost feel his arms around us and I reached out with my own arms.

But instead of Da, Patch had come along in back of me, the bottom of his skirt dragging. He put one hand in mine and pointed with the other. "Sean Red there."

I saw him too, going over the road, his brothers with him. They carried the currach over their heads so that only their legs showed beneath them. The currach looked like a great black beetle inching itself toward the sea.

"They're on their way to catch fish." I wondered if I could go with them someday. Would there be room? I'd work hard, I'd tell them, if they'd give me a place and a bit of the catch to take home.

I wasn't good with the oars and they all knew it.

"Nory." Patch tugged on my arm. "I have the hunger."

"I know it," I said. "But you will be strong." I tried to think. "Strong as Cuchulain, the great warrior."

He shook his head hard. "I just want my nice potato."

I bent down and rocked him. "Your eyes are leaking tears," I said.

He tried to smile, looking down, his eyelashes long on his cheeks.

"I am hungry too," I said. "But we won't think about it. We'll go to Anna's."

"And she will give us milk from the cow?"

I shook my head. "She needs her own milk."

"Then why are we going there?"

"I will help her." I squeezed his hand.

In the distance, the rocks glittered on the hills; it seemed as if a soft green cloth was stretched over them. I saw another world up there, clean and fresh smelling, but with nothing to feed any of us.

Patch pointed at a gannet flying up overhead, its neck reaching. He began the saying: *"One to be sad."*

We waited for a second bird. *"Two to be glad,"* I said.

Patch was smiling. *"Three to get married,"* he said as the third bird caught up with the other two.

And then we were at Anna's open door. "Do you want me to milk the cow?" I called in.

"I have milked my own cow." She came outside, shading her eyes against the sun.

"Then what will I do?"

She reached out, pointing to the fields. "They will strip the land," she said.

"Who?"

"Everyone who is hungry."

"I am hungry," Patch said. "I am very hungry."

She went inside her house and was back a moment later with a small wooden bowl in her hand. It was half filled with milk. "Drink slowly," she told him.

A tap of pain in back of my eyes. Milk almost yellow with cream.

She tipped the bowl into Patch's mouth and he drank it all. She stared at me, knowing I wanted a bowl of it too, knowing I wouldn't ask. "You are stronger than you think," she said.

I put out my chin. "I am not hungry," I said. "But thank you for the milk for Patch."

She nodded. "Come with me now. We will gather nettles and dandelion leaves." She nodded to herself. "Onions for insect bites, ivy for burns."

With her cane in one hand and a basket in the other, she didn't even try to stay away from the clumps of mush on the ground. Bits of black and brown with white spreading across . . .

*Fuafar.*

We followed her to the cemetery first. We didn't have to tell Patch to stay away from the nettles. "They sting," he said, and waited at the edge of the small path.

Anna had rags in her basket to wrap around our hands. I looked across at my mam's grave. She'd know what to do about potatoes and coins.

"My husband is there." Anna pointed her toe at a bit of ground.

Anna had a husband?

"My son with him," she said.

A little boy?

I must have said it aloud because Anna shook her head. "A man, grown."

How had I not known that? Maggie must have known, and Granda. Maybe I had never listened. A husband. A son.

Anna was ahead of me, pulling the nettles carefully so they wouldn't sting. I followed her slowly and began to pull the nettles with her. I was hungry, so hungry.

I thought about the potatoes we had gathered yesterday. *Just get through this day without food,* I told myself. Tonight Celia would have the potatoes bubbling in the pot and we'd go to bed with our stomachs filled.

I began to sing with Patch. Anna, still bent over the nettles, turned her head. It almost seemed as if she smiled. But that couldn't be. I had never seen Anna Donnelly smile.

# Chapter 11

That night I dreamed, half awake, half sleeping. I'd sit up, eyeing the crack under the door, wondering if it was morning, worrying about being late. Then I'd fall back, remembering what Anna had taught me. *Wild garlic and honey for coughs. Leaves, stems, and roots of selfheal, watered and stirred into a* fuafar *froth and strained.*

Was that for fever? I tried to remember. Anna must have told me dozens of cures, stuffing them into my head the way you'd stuff the potatoes into a rush bowl.

Potatoes. *Don't think about potatoes,* I told myself, and turned over, the straw rustling under me.

The next morning I was up earlier than I had ever been. I said my prayers as I went, not taking time to kneel next to the bed. I had to be at Mallons' house before their rooster crowed.

I wasn't so hungry now. Strange because we had gone to bed with headaches and stomachaches, and Patch crying the way he had while Maggie walked away to Galway port. I sang an old song of Da's to comfort him until Celia threw a handful of bed straw at me, and Granda told us to say our prayers and close our eyes.

Now I crossed the field, watching for the Mallon brothers. I had to be sure they wouldn't get themselves down to the strand before I reached them.

I thought about last night, coming in through the open door, my wrist stinging from one of the long nettles, but hardly paying attention to it, mouth watering over the potatoes that Celia would be cooking.

"It was a good plan, Granda," I'd said, "we're through the day and it's time for a meal."

But Celia had shaken her head. The small pile of potatoes we had picked so carefully seemed shrunken and the spots had spread and run into each other, leaving ridges of black. Celia bit her lip. "We have to get rid of these," she said. "We can't eat them."

"We'll cut the spots out," I said. "We'll do it carefully, then we'll boil the good parts."

"Do you suppose they'll make us sick?" Celia asked.

"We have to try," Granda said.

Celia looked at Muc in her corner pen. "We'll give her a wee bite first, and see what happens."

"I'm glad I'm not the pig." I reached for the first potato and the knife that swung on its hook and began to cut. It took a long time. The potatoes were small to begin with and when I was finished the pile would fit in Patch's cap.

We boiled what we had anyway, but there was no need to test them out on Muc. In front of our eyes, the bubbling water turned dark and the same dreadful smell from the fields was on us.

After Celia had thrown the whole mess out in the yard, pot, water, and praties, we'd gone down to Cunningham's stream. We'd taken a bowl of his water and a few of his leaves back to boil for a bit of soup.

But there was no time now to daydream about yesterday. The Mallon brothers were just ahead of me under their currach. I called out to them and the muffled sound of their "Hello" came back across the field.

I ran toward them. "Let me come with you."

They didn't stop.

"I won't take up much room," I told them. "I'll sit on the bottom, between the seats. All I need is a line and a hook."

They moved away from me. Michael's voice came from under the currach. "There's no room, Nory, and you don't know how to fish beyond the surf."

"Please," I said. "Please."

74

I could hear Liam, too. "Ah, Nory," he was saying, "ah."

Was he feeling sorry for me?

Suddenly I was angry. Angrier than I could ever remember. I picked up a stone and threw it as hard as I could. It bounced off the currach with a small thud.

"What was that?" Michael asked.

"Let me come," I called, but they angled the currach up and over the stile and started down the path toward the strand. I walked in back of them all the way, yelling, wanting to cry the way Patch had last night.

At last they took pity on me. They rested the currach on their hands and ducked their heads so I could see their faces. "Nory Ryan," said Michael, "I know you are hungry. We are all hungry."

"Let me . . . ," I began again, but I could see by their faces that the answer was no.

"Listen," Liam said, "wait here for Sean. He is coming soon, to pick up the limpets and the mussels along the shore."

"Limpets," I said. *Fuafar.*

"If you are hungry enough you will eat them." Michael blew his red hair out of his eyes. "And I think before we are finished, we will be glad to have even that."

I didn't say another word. I was still angry, and besides that, I needed a pail.

"Go up to the house," Liam said, knowing what I was thinking. "Someone will give you a pail."

They grunted with the weight of the currach as they went along the sandy path, but I didn't waste time watching them. I turned and walked up to the door of the Mallon house. "Bless all here," I called in through the open doorway.

Granny Mallon sat on her heels near the fire smoking her pipe, and Mrs. Mallon was at the hearth. They both nodded. "*Dia duit,* Nora."

"Is Sean here?" I began. "And could I have a pail, please?"

Mrs. Mallon jerked her thumb over her shoulder. "A pail outside, and Sean around the back of the house."

I could see how hungry Sean was as I turned the corner. He had always been skinny, but overnight the color had gone from his face, and his eyes were huge, like Patch's. "We will catch us some *fuafar* limpets," I said. "And some black mussels, too."

He smiled at me, patting his pockets, looking for dulse, I knew. Then we started for the path to the beach. I loved this path. As the path turned one way, we'd see a bit of the sea, and then as it wandered another, the sea would be lost and the grass would be high as our heads, and blowing with the sound of whispers, music just for us.

As we went down, the cliffs in back of us rose higher and higher, and the gannets and kestrels wheeled and dipped. I thought that Brooklyn, New York, America, could not have been as beautiful even with its diamond streets.

We were at the last turn now. I knew what I'd see next: the sea stretched out in front of us, waves crashing onto our little strand, with not a soul in sight except for the Mallons as they ran into the surf with the currach.

I stopped at the end of the path, my mouth open. The strand was filled with people. People I never saw at the water's edge. People I saw only during the time of the fair. They had walked a long way to get here. Some gathered seaweed and the others looked for limpets and mussels.

Our mussels.

Our *fuafar* limpets.

Sean and I looked at each other. "Hurry," he said.

We began to run, the sand dragging at our feet. At the water's edge we started to dig, getting into everyone's way, splashing, the sand under our nails and crushed shells

77

biting at our feet. Around us people called to each other.

Suddenly it was silent, as silent as it could be with the waves running high and throwing themselves up on the rocks at our feet.

What was happening?

I looked first at the currach. It was just beyond the waves now, and Liam and Michael were bent over the oars.

Next to me a woman held a small clump of black mussels, her skirt soaked with spray. Her mouth opened as she turned, staring.

I swiveled around, shading my eyes. Lord Cunningham on a huge white horse was coming toward us from the bottom of the path.

My heart jumped, even though I knew it was all right to be there. It was not Lord Cunningham's beach, after all. It was not his ocean.

Still, I knew there'd be trouble.

He shouted as he pounded across the strand toward us, the sand spewing up in great circles.

Cunningham rode into the surf so that the horse was in water up to his knees, and the sea licked at the lord's boots. "You!" he shouted at the currach, waving his riding crop over his head. "Come back."

Next to me Sean shook his head, his face and hair peppered with sand.

The Mallons stopped rowing, their oars raised, and Cunningham rode another few feet into the surf. Michael said something; I could see the anger on his face. Then Liam dipped his oars into the water again. They began to row toward the shore, riding in on a wave, and Sean ran to help them beach the currach.

"What is it?" Sean asked. "What?"

Around me the women were backing away, so there was a space between us. In the middle of the space were Cunningham, the horse, and the currach at the water's edge.

"The currach belongs to me now," Cunningham screamed. "To me."

# Chapter 12

I was still on the beach later that day, gathering limpets. Sean and his brothers were gone.

The currach was gone too, gone to pay for the Mallons' rent from last year. Gone, not even for Cunningham to use. "What would he want with the sea, and the cold, and the aching hard work?" Liam had said. "What would he want with the danger?"

Devlin had locked it up with chains on the pier in the harbor. It would be there, with the tar on the canvas drying and cracking, until great holes appeared and the currach wasted away. It wouldn't be the first time. There were others there, waiting for the owners to pay the rent they owed and get them back, but it never happened.

But I couldn't think of the currach now. I had to eat something right away. I couldn't wait for the hen that Celia would cook.

I didn't even want to think about the hen. What we were doing would not be a good idea in the end. It would mean one less egg every day. I imagined a mountain of eggs, each of them sizzling in a little pan, gone like Mallons' currach.

And then I thought about the limpets sloshing around in a pail of seawater. Slimy. Cold. Poor people's food, we called them. Last hope.

It was milk I wanted, a sea of milk with great lumps of potatoes, an ocean of milk to drink until I was full.

Anna.

Would she trade me a cup of milk for the limpets in my pail?

I ducked into Anna's doorway, thinking about the first time I had gone into her house. I had edged my way into the dimness, peering into the corners, ready to run if I saw one of the *sidhe,* her hair long, her fingers bony, watching me.

But Anna's house was like ours: a hearth with banked-up ashes, a bed of straw, a three-legged stool. There was more, a table covered with dried pieces of moss and buttercups. Tiny bits of faded green and brown from the plants around Maidin Bay.

I set the pail of limpets down on the floor. *"Dia duit."*

Without my asking, she lifted the pail of milk in the corner. A small pail, with milk in the bottom. She poured it into a wooden cup.

The milk still had a bit of froth on top. It was creamy with bits of yellow fat, even though the cow was thin as a rail.

I closed my eyes. Suddenly I felt weak. If I had to watch her put the cup to her mouth and drink that milk, I would lie down on the floor and not get up again.

Anna stopped pouring, then looked at the cup. She poured in a bit more until the milk was almost to the top. A sea of white surrounded by the rim of the cup . . .

. . . and she gave it to me, holding my hands with her own, lifting the cup to my mouth. I had never tasted anything better. Leaves of dulse, a bit of meat shredded into soup on Christmas Day, the sticky red candy that Da had bought us after the harvest one year were nothing like this sweet milk.

I didn't stop drinking until the cup was empty and I began to think about Anna's dry hands holding mine. She was so small I had to look down at her, down at the little white cap on her head, the thick creases across her forehead, the faded blue eyes in the folds of skin.

I ran my tongue over my lips, feeling the last drops of milk as she took the cup and hung it on a hook over the hearth.

How could I ever have been afraid of her?

"The *madra* is gone," she said.

"Gone? Maeve? How could that be?"

Maeve with her ears flying, her tail waving. Maeve protecting us at Cunningham's stream.

"I don't know what happened to her."

How sad Anna looked. She shook her head, then went to the table to chop a pile of nettles. "These will make a good soup," she said.

"The Mallons lost their currach."

She looked up at me quickly. "Because of the shed they built?" she asked. "Devlin raised the rent. They couldn't pay."

"Yes."

"And it may be that they will lose their house."

I nodded. No currach meant no fish. If they couldn't sell the fish or eat the fish . . . It was too much to think about.

Anna was leaning on the end of the table, her stick propped up next to her. "The English want us out of here." She raised one shoulder. "They want our land for sheep, they want it for themselves. You will see. They will offer little help when we starve this winter. They will put us out on the road without a care."

"You sound like Granda," I said.

"Yes." Her back was toward me now. She reached for bits of green, mixing them with something else. "This is good for toothaches," she said, staring up at the bottle as she filled it.

By that time I remembered the limpets floating around in the pail by the doorway. And I owed these to Anna too, for the milk. I went outside and came back with the pail, water sloshing.

One hand on the table, she pushed at the pail with one bare toe: greenish brown water, a few strands of sea grass, and limpets moving gently.

"*Fuafar*," she said, and we both laughed.

"They are for you," I said.

She looked at me, eyes narrowed. "My son, Tague . . ."

"He was the cliff fisherman," I said, suddenly realizing.

"He would go down on the strand and bring back . . ."

I leaned forward to listen, thinking about the story of Tague. A rope slung around his waist, whipping out and out and down. And because he reached out too far, the wind had pulled him off the cliff.

Anna stopped speaking and put up her hand. I heard it too. Voices calling. Voices calling, "Nory."

"Nor-rrrrrrry." That was Celia.

"Nor-rrrrry." Sean Red.

"Nor-rrrry." Even Patch.

Something was wrong. Was it Granda? I backed away from Anna at the table.

"Take the limpets," Anna said.

I shook my head. "For you."

"I have enough," she said.

"Nory." One voice started as soon as the other had stopped. Sean's the deepest. Celia's a little higher. Patch's baby voice.

I picked up the pail by the wire handle and ducked out the doorway, waving my other hand so they could see me across the field. But when they did, they started to run. "Hurry," they called.

I followed them, leaving the pail in back of the stone wall where no one could find it. Then I flew across the field so I could catch them before they turned down to our house. But instead they were following the road to Ballilee.

# Chapter 13

"A package," Celia said when I caught up to them. Her nose twitched with excitement. "In the post office."

"From Maggie?" I took a breath. "It must be." We had never gotten something from the post office, not once in our whole lives.

"Michael Mallon was there in Ballilee," Celia said, "and they told him."

We looked at each other, Celia reaching out so our hands met.

It was a long walk and the road was stony. We kept to the edge to walk on the soft weeds that grew next to the hedges. As the road twisted we caught glimpses of the sea below, and the strand still filled with people.

More people I didn't know. People who didn't live in Maidin Bay or even nearby.

*"They will strip the earth,"* Anna had said.

And the sea, I thought, watching fishermen jog each other as they tried for a catch with ropes and bits of string. Granda said there was a world just like ours on the bottom of the sea where the *sidhe* planted potatoes in the sand and drank tea from tiny shell cups. Horses galloped past their houses on the way to a sea city. Granda had said if you bent your ear to the water on a dark night, you might hear the horses neighing.

I'd always meant to bend my ear to it. I stood there for a moment until Celia tugged at my arm. "Hurry," she said.

At the top of a small hill Ballilee spread out before us. The church, the rectory, a row of houses; and in back of the hotel, someone emptied a pail of dirty water. A crowd of people had gathered in front of the bakery. They were begging for food. Some were mothers with tiny babies in their arms.

Babies with big eyes.

Celia hesitated. I took her arm. "Try not to look."

We had never been inside the post office. Could we walk in by ourselves? We peered in the window at Brennan, the postman, in back of the counter. Another man was there too, gathering a pile of envelopes for the hotel.

Patch was the brave one. Before we could stop him, he pushed open the door and was inside. Sean was next, looking back over his shoulder at us.

I put my head in the air so Celia wouldn't think I was afraid and sailed inside in back of the other two.

"There is something for us," I said.

Mr. Brennan looked across the counter. "A package."

"Yes," Celia breathed.

Maggie. Maggie had sent us something all the way from Brooklyn, New York. Mr. Brennan pointed to a box on the shelf. It was scribbled over with writing; bits of colored paper were stuck to it.

What was inside? What could it be? I tried to think. Could Maggie have pried diamonds out of the Brooklyn streets? Did the diamonds belong to everyone? Could you do that? Would we be rich?

I'd give Anna a coin straightaway, and more besides, much more. I'd get back the Mallons' currach and tell Liam I was doing it for him even though he hadn't let me come with him. I'd buy Patch penny candy and Granda a jar of *poitín*. But first I'd buy food. We'd eat and eat.

But maybe the box held warm things to wear. Granda was cold all the time. And a shawl for me, one with fringe. Red it would be, my favorite color.

Or food.

I had to laugh at myself for thinking of that, laugh as I felt my stomach folding itself together, so hungry. What food could be sent all that way and still be good inside the package?

No, I was back to diamonds. That was what I'd hope for.

But Mr. Brennan didn't reach for the package. He looked out the window at the people gathered in front of the bakery. They were begging, yelling for food. Someone threw a rock through the window, and the people climbed in over the broken glass. The baker, a cut on his cheek, slipped out his door. Then he was outside, running down the street, away from his rolls, and his bread, and his penny buns.

In a moment everything was gone. The shelves were bare, and outside the people tore loaves of bread into chunks, fighting over them, trampling each other.

Celia and I backed up against the wall. Patch buried his head in my skirt. And even Sean Red stood there, hands dangling, his eyes wide.

I rubbed my fingers over Patch's back, feeling the bones, tiny as Biddy the hen's. "Don't be afraid," I whispered, trying not to let him feel my hands shake.

The police came, three of them with clubs and whistles. But there was no one to arrest. They had disappeared up the street and into the alleys.

I turned back to Mr. Brennan. "Our package, please." I didn't dare hold out my hand, but I asked in a determined voice, as if I received a package from Brooklyn, New York, America, every day.

But Mr. Brennan shook his head.

"You said it was ours." What would happen if I reached across the counter, and grabbed it, and ran?

At last he took the box down. I tried to see by the way he handled it . . . was it heavy enough to be holding diamonds? They could be small ones, tiny ones. I began to smile.

But he showed us the bits of colored paper. "Not enough stamps," he said. "There's money due on this."

I shook my head. "I don't understand."

Celia moved forward. "It is for the Ryans," she said. "For Granda and Nory and me. It's from Maggie. You know that."

He raised one shoulder just the slightest bit. "You'll have to pay what's owing."

I shook my head. "We don't have coins; we have no money."

And as we said it, he slid the package back across the counter. I reached out and touched it, and the paper slid away under my fingers, the paper and the bits of colored pictures. I almost caught it by the string, but then, in the blink of an eye, it was up on the shelf.

"That is not right." My voice was quivering and my chin unsteady. How cruel he was. Worse than Devlin. Worse than the English. "That's ours," I said. "Ours from Maggie."

And then I saw his eyes, and I knew he was sorry for us.

"I will hold it for you," he said, leaning toward us. "I will keep it here on the shelf. As soon as you get some money . . ."

"It will be forever," I said.

"I will keep it here for you forever, then," he said.

We stood looking up at the package, Celia, Sean Red, Patch, and I. Celia was crying. I tried to say something to make her smile. "Tear bag," I said, but I could hardly get the words out.

"What is inside?" Patch was asking. "Is it something to eat?"

Someone else came into the post office, and Mr. Brennan made motions with his hands, telling us to go.

We walked home slowly. Slowly because I was still trying to think of a way to get the package. Slowly because it had started to rain, a cold fall rain, and the road had turned to mud. Slowly because we were so hungry.

# Chapter 14

The next day was Sunday. We walked halfway to Ballilee to the church for Mass. It took longer than usual. Now that we had the hunger, we moved slowly. On the altar, Father Harte moved slowly too. When he turned toward us, holding out his arms for the Kyrie, his hands trembled; his face was pale and thin.

We prayed for someone to help, prayed for the English to give up the rents this year, and then we came home. We made ourselves a meal of one poor hen. She was old and tough but we ate every shred of meat and sucked on the bones until they fell apart in our mouths. We made sure Patch had the softest whitest bits we could find. We didn't dare look at Biddy and the second sister, who scratched around on the floor beside us.

"Do you think they know?" Celia asked.

"I don't even care." It was the first time my stomach had been full since the potatoes had failed.

But Granda said, "We can't do this again." He looked almost desperate. "We have lost an egg a day that would have kept us alive. We must keep the other two hens carefully, and find seed for them somehow."

Celia and I nodded, ashamed because we hadn't even felt sorry for the sister we had just eaten. We had been sorry only that she hadn't had more meat on her bones.

Granda cleared his throat, looking up the way he always did. "They are building a road around Maidin Bay."

"A road?" I sucked on the end of a bone, licking my fingers.

"For what reason?" Celia said.

Granda raised a shoulder in the air. "For no reason. The English will have us build roads that go nowhere. They will give us money but in the end they want nothing to be better."

"We are going to build a road?" *How could I ever build a road?* I wondered.

"Not you," Granda said. "Of course not you. How could you break up rocks and carry them?"

"Oh," I said, relieved.

"Me," said Granda.

Celia rolled her eyes at me.

"I will start tomorrow morning," Granda said.

"No." I swallowed a piece of bone, feeling the sharp edges in my throat.

Granda smoothed down his beard. "It is the only way."

Celia bit her lips. They were chapped, so dry they were cracked and bleeding. I'd ask Anna what to do about it. She was trying to put every one of her cures into my head. A bit of boiled fish for sores. Garlic for sore throat. Egg white for . . . I couldn't remember what. Even warm cow dung for burns. *Fuafar*.

Granda started again. "The rent will be due again soon."

I closed my eyes. The rain was so much colder now and the damp seeped through our clothes. We hadn't paid the last of the old rent, and soon the new one would be on us.

I pictured Da coming along the road, his pack on his shoulders, and felt a pain in my chest. He should have been here by now.

Suppose something had happened to him? How would we know?

"They will give us a little money." Granda spread his hands wide. "And a meal at the end of the day."

"The work is too hard for you," Celia said. She scooped up the bones and put them into the pot for a broth.

Granda leaned forward. "The money will help feed the three of you. It will buy milk or a piece of salmon if there's any to be had in

Ballilee. You won't have to worry about me."

Not worry? Granda chopping up rocks, laying them out on a road no one needed?

Celia stood up. She licked one finger and worked at a stain on her skirt.

"Tell Granda he can't do this," I said, but Celia was looking at her feet. "I wish I had shoes," she whispered.

"Celia. What about Granda?"

"I will give them a wash," she said. "That's the best I can do."

I was furious. "Will you pay attention to me!"

"I'm off to see Lord Cunningham," she said. "I'll ask for a job in the kitchen. I'm a good cook. I wish I had thought of it sooner."

"You are a *fuafar* cook. And that's a terrible . . ." I began to say "idea." But it wasn't a terrible idea. It was the best idea any of us had had in a long time. I thought of Maggie on the cliff the day she left. *Celia is loyal and true.*

Celia went to the shelf for her piece of the comb. Broken in half, it hardly smoothed her hair at all. "How do I look?" she asked.

"Like a goat. A little nanny goat." I took the comb from her and gently ran it through her hair, teasing out the knots.

Celia took a quick look at the closed door. None of us had ever been on the road after dark. We knew the *sidhe* were out there. She shook herself. "You are not to move from your place at the hearth, Granda. You will stay here, *a stór,* and I will cook up a mess of food at Cunningham's, and bring potatoes in buttermilk for you and a sour little limpet for my sour little sister."

I raised my hand to my mouth. "I forgot them. Here we are starving and the limpets are swimming around in their pail behind the stone wall outside. They must think they're arrived in a strange wee ocean."

Celia and Granda looked at each other, wondering, I guessed, if I had lost my mind.

"The ones I left there." I waved my hand. "I'll get them."

I'd have to go out in the dark too.

"A delicious treat," I whispered to give myself courage.

I said it to Celia's back. She stood with both feet in the bowl on the floor, sloshing them up and down, looking at her toes. "I'll never get the poor things clean," she said, "not unless I spend a month in this spot." She shook one foot, spraying dirty water around. "The *sidhe* will hate this water." She tried to smile. She stood at the door for a moment, looking back at us. I knew she was afraid too.

I nodded at her to show I thought she was brave, and then she was gone.

"I will go for the limpets," I said. I didn't want Granda to know I was just as afraid as Celia. And I didn't even have that far to go. Across the field and halfway to Anna's house. I went to the doorway. There was no moon tonight and the fields were dark. I could see a tallow light at Mallons' house, but none in Anna's window. I shivered.

"I will go to the road tomorrow even so," Granda said as if he were arguing with me. "My hands are still strong, and my back. You will see. I will bring money home and we will last, the four of us, until your da comes home."

I didn't answer him. I'd wait until Celia came home. The two of us would make sure he did no such thing.

I stepped from the doorway into the dark world. For all I knew ghostly gray men were out there waiting for me. I had heard they made themselves into wisps of fog, ugly and unfriendly to humans. Or maybe I'd see a *bean sídhe* with her hair flowing, moaning because someone was going to die.

Something moved in the field, and I

began to sing Granda's old war song for courage.

I thought of Patch and pretended I was holding his warm little hand. I imagined we were out to gather stones for his wall, that the sliver of moon was a bit of the sun, and I started to run. Where was that pail? I went the length of the wall, searching, so hungry my mouth was watering for those limpets.

Who would have stolen them?

I almost fell over the pail on its side, water spilled, the limpets hard little lumps.

A voice from so long ago. *You never think. You never finish what you start.*

"Oh, Celia, *a stór,* you are right," I said, scooping up the mess that no one could eat.

# Chapter 15

Celia came back that dark night and slid onto the straw of our bed without stopping to kneel for her prayers. She didn't say a word to me but twisted and turned, pulling our covers one way and then another. I thought we'd never get to sleep.

Days later she told me Cunningham had laughed at her feet without shoes, and the stain on her dress. "You won't be here long enough to work," he had said. "You'll be out of your house and onto the road because you cannot last, and I will see sheep grazing where your house had been."

I knew I'd never forget the terrible look in her eyes. "Celia," I said. "Do you know what Maggie said about you?"

She shook her head.

I put my hand on her thin shoulder. "She said you are loyal and true. And that is what I say. No one could ever ask for more."

She blinked, trying not to let the tears fall. "I always worried," she said. "Worried when it rained that the thatch would leak, worried when the sun was hot that the thatch would burn." She brushed the back of her hand over her face. "But if we live through this,

I'll never worry about things like that again."

"You might even sing," I said, trying to change what I saw in her eyes.

"A rusty gate, I am." And then she patted my hand on her shoulder. "I saw the dog," she said slowly. "The dog you gave to Anna. She's penned up in a cage with the other hunting dogs."

"Anna loves Maeve!" Before I could say anything else, Granda came through the door to tell us the road people had sent him away too. It was only Sean Red who would be working on the road, Sean because he was tall and looked older than he was.

Liam and Michael were leaving Maidin Bay to walk to the port of Galway. They'd leave without a penny between them, with only the clothes on their backs. "We must have a ship to fish," Michael had told Granda. "Or a ship to sail. We will go wherever it takes us. Our shoulders are broad enough to find work on the way."

Again we walked to the crossroads. Mrs. Mallon's face, always red, was blotched and swollen. This time Patch and I were the only Ryans going with them. Granda had started a cough and Celia stayed with him to give him some of the cure I had made with Anna's garlic. Poor Sean was off on the road, breaking up huge chunks of rock.

We waved at the brothers until they turned the corner; then Devlin came along on his horse.

"We have taken down the shed," old Granny Mallon told him. "You will see, if you look, that it is gone."

"You have ruined the property?" he said. "Lord Cunningham's property, Lord Cunningham's shed?"

"What?" Old Granny looked dazed.

Mrs. Mallon pulled her away as we looked up at him. How could he be so cruel? We backed up against the edge of the road as he rode past us, the horse's hooves spewing mud and clay.

We walked slowly. Mrs. Mallon weaved back and forth on the path, trying to hold old Granny up. She looked as old as Granny herself, with sunken cheeks and loose gray flesh.

And Patch couldn't keep up either. His arms were like sticks and his legs white and bowed where they hung out of his skirt. "Come, Patcheen," I said. "We have to go home."

Instead of hurrying, he sank down on the ground and put his arms out to me.

People walked around him. That was another thing, the people. Where had they

101

come from? They wandered along the roads in twos and threes. They were mostly women carrying babies. Little children held on to their skirts.

It was such an effort to walk to Patch, to put my arms around him and pick him up. And when I did, there was nothing to him. All we'd been eating were the few fish we'd managed to poach from Cunningham's stream and once in a while a wild onion or an old potato. I sank down next to Patch on the wet ground and watched the people. Some of them had circles of green around their mouths.

I wondered what it was.

I wondered how I could get some.

And then I knew. "They are eating grass," I told Patch.

"Me," he said. "I will have grass."

I stood up again and looked at the sea grass that bent itself over the rocky road. I pulled a piece up and put it in my mouth. "Sharp enough to cut your tongue," I told Patch. I pulled another piece off for him. "Be careful."

He leaned against a rock, and I leaned back with him. We lay there, sucking on the blades of grass. Clouds rushed against the blue of the sky, changing shapes as we looked. "There," I said. "That looks like the cat Mallons had once."

Patch looked up too. "Yes — Lizzie."

The Lizzie shape turned into a pig. Muc. Muc hadn't had anything to eat except for the grass around the house. She looked thinner every day. *Don't think about that,* I told myself.

"I wonder if these same clouds get to Brooklyn." I pictured Maggie looking up, seeing the cat in the clouds, and Muc, and maybe even me.

Maggie.

*Brooklyn. Horses clopping. Milk in cans. No one hungry.*

Liam could build a shed for himself if he got there, and it would be his own.

Across the fields was Anna's house. Suddenly I realized there was no smoke coming from the roof. I held my face up to feel the wind. The smoke should have been drifting toward me. I pulled myself up and waited until a bit of dizziness passed.

Next to me, Patch was asleep now, his thumb in his mouth.

"Stay then, and rest," I whispered. "I will come back for you."

The walk across the field seemed much longer than usual. I stumbled against the potato plants, dry now, stiff, crumbling underneath me. Then I was at Anna's door.

Her cow was nowhere in sight; neither was her pig. "Anna," I called, feeling my lips crack. They had been as sore as Celia's for days now. I ducked inside to see Anna lying in her straw bed, stiff and unmoving.

For a moment I felt as if I couldn't breathe; then she turned toward me. "Are you all right?" I asked.

"An old woman can lie in her bed if she wishes," she said. "And there's milk. I saved it for you."

My mouth watered. "I didn't come for milk." I wanted it so much I felt weak.

"I've had so much milk today," Anna said, "I couldn't drink another drop."

"Well then, I will," I said. "And if you don't mind, I'll take a wee drop for Patch."

I went to the pail in the corner. I was too weak to lift it and pour some into a cup, and there wasn't that much in the pail anyway. I bent over and tipped until I felt the warmth of it on my tongue. I had to make myself stop. Patch was so hungry on the road, and Anna . . .

"Did you really have enough to drink?" I asked.

Her eyes were closed but I could see her nod.

"Where is your cow?" I said next, still tasting the milk.

"I sent her away this day."

I went closer. "Sent your cow away? What do you mean? Sold her?"

"Gave . . ."

"Gave her to . . ." I repeated, and then I knew. "Devlin?"

She made a small sound. "I cured his stomachache with a blackberry root, but he forgot that."

I leaned closer. "Devlin took her for the rent?" I swallowed. All the milk would be gone now. What would Anna eat? "And the pig? Did he take the pig?"

She didn't answer. She turned again, the straw settling under her. I stood there, heart pounding, remembering the coin. It would have paid the rent.

I took a wooden cup and poured a mouthful into it. I knelt by her bed with it until she turned her head and drank. "You are a good girl," she said.

I blurted it out then. "Your coin didn't even help to save the Neelys," I said. "I dropped it into the well."

She reached out with both her hands and put them on my cheeks. "The well, but why?"

I spread out my hands. "I thought the bailiff was in back of me, but it was only the dog."

"The dog," Anna said.

I couldn't tell her where the dog was. Instead I sat there staring at the fire. "When Da comes home . . . ," I began. "I haven't forgotten. We will give the coin to you first. Somehow."

Anna leaned forward. She traced the line of my chin with her hand. "We will talk about this," she said. "I have things to say to you. But now you must take the milk to Patch."

I hooked the pail's handle under my fingers and went to the door with it. "I know so much about the plants now." I stopped, looking down at the milk. "I'll never forget." I'd be like Anna now, able to heal.

"And something else," I said. "I will never leave you. I will stay with you always, and take care of you."

She raised her head, smiled, and shook her head the slightest bit.

I took the pail to the end of the field, glancing around to be sure no one on the road might take it away from me. I kept calling until at last Patch raised his head and came to me across the wall.

# Chapter 16

After Patch finished the milk we ran our fingers around the inside of the pail, licking each finger until there was nothing left. I began to think. If Devlin had taken Anna's cow and her pig, if Devlin had come for the rent . . .

What about our rent, and Da not home with the money?

What about Muc? What about Biddy and her sister?

I left the pail on its side. I took Patch's hand. "We must go home, *a stór*," I told him. "We must go quickly."

We went down the road, Patch dragging his feet. My own legs felt like pieces of lumber that had washed up in the surf: numb and heavy. But somehow we crossed the stony field to our doorway.

Granda was on the floor, rooting through one of the baskets, mumbling to himself. Celia was kneeling at the hearth, blowing on the turf. No one else was there. I leaned against the doorway, holding my side, trying to catch my breath. They looked up. Celia's nose twitched — a sign she was going to say something I didn't like. "I'm going to kill Biddy's sister," she said. "She hasn't laid an egg in days. She doesn't have enough to eat."

My mouth watered. *Poor sister.* I couldn't help it.

Granda glanced up at me, waiting for me to say it wasn't a good idea. But I couldn't. He went back to rooting in the basket and pulled out an old frieze jacket. "Warm enough for this weather," he said, brushing it.

I hardly paid attention. "Devlin hasn't been here then," I said.

Granda stopped brushing and Celia turned away from the hearth, still on her heels.

"He took Anna's cow," I said. "And her pig."

Celia rubbed her hands on her skirt. "We have to count on Muc and the piglets to come."

"Six piglets," Patch said.

"We don't have the money for the rent," I said, shaking my head.

"If only Da were here." Celia lowered her head. "Was he ever this late in coming?"

He'd always come by this time, I thought. "If he could be anywhere, he'd want to be here."

"I know that," she said. "Do you think something has happened?"

I didn't want to answer. The ship might have foundered. He could have starved on the road. He could be sick.

Granda sat, thinking. "When Devlin comes, you will ask him for a few days," he said. "I will go to Galway to find your father."

Celia said, "I will go."

Just then we heard the horse coming down the road. My hands began to shake. With one movement, Celia grabbed up Biddy's sister and was out the door with Patch in back of her. She darted around the side of the house, holding on to the hen. I shooed Biddy out, but there wasn't time to do anything about Muc.

At the doorway I watched the horse come closer. Devlin was on his way from the Mallons', coming toward us. Outside Biddy's sister clucked, more than clucked, screeched. Inside I heard Granda fall over something, metal clattering against the stones of the hearth, Granda groaning.

Devlin wheeled the horse around, dust flying. "I've come for the rent," he said.

I hardly paid attention to him. I went back into the house to Granda. He pulled himself to his feet and I reached for him, holding him tight.

Devlin had followed me inside. "You know why I'm here."

"My da . . ." I could hardly speak. "He's fishing out of Galway. As soon as —"

"The rent is due, and half from last time."

I shook my head.

"I will tumble the house and put you out on the road," he said. "But for now I will have the pig and the hen." He walked back to the doorway, his hands sweeping over the field.

By the mercy of God the other hen had stopped screeching.

"You will still owe the rent." He glanced across the yard at poor Biddy pecking on something, at Muc trying to find a blade of grass to ease her hunger. He pulled a small book out from under his cape and wrote something in it. "Bring them to the dock. They'll have a sea trip to England."

Then he was on his horse again, following the road away from us. Granda sat down heavily in front of the fire, and Celia appeared with scratches on her face and hands.

"You saved the hen," I said, and ran my hand along her reddened cheek. "You are a great girl, *a stór*."

"And you," she said, "you as well."

That afternoon, I thought, was the saddest in my life. "Send the sister off," I told Celia. "We will keep Biddy."

"Eat Biddy?" Celia asked, shocked.

"Never," I said.

She nodded. "That is why we must keep the sister and let Biddy go."

I knew what she was saying. If we did not eat soon, how could we go on?

We made a meal of the sister, closing the door tightly, hoping that no one would come. Still, I saved two morsels for Anna. I would have saved a third for Sean Red because he would have done that for me, but they had sent him down to work on a road near the bay and I didn't know when he would be back.

When the poor little meal was finished, Granda stood up. "I will go down to Galway to find your father before it is too late."

Once his mind was made up, neither of us could change it. Celia and I stared at each other, thinking of what had to be done. I spoke first. "Celia will go with you. She is older and stronger."

Words I would never have said before. And what I didn't say was that staying in this house alone at night with Patch was the worst thing I could think of and I couldn't do that to Celia.

"And Nory will watch out for Patch." Celia bit her lip. "She will wait on the chance that we miss Da."

Only one road went to Galway, and it wound along the coast like a ball of yarn let loose, Da had said. "You won't miss him if he's there," I told her. "Just stay on the road."

Celia and I stared at each other. We knew we might never be together again. "I will hear you singing always," she said.

They left early the next morning, moving slowly enough for me to take the comb out of the basket and run after Celia with both pieces. "Take it," I said. "Keep it, half yours and half mine."

"I know why you said you'd stay," she said, taking one of the pieces and pressing the other into my hand. "I will never forget it."

I wanted to tell her I remembered that day we had broken the comb, remembered her staring at Patch's bed and deciding not to take the road to Galway. If she had, I thought, she wouldn't be taking this terrible trip now. She'd be in Brooklyn, America, safe. I couldn't say that, though. I'd never get the words out. I ducked my head. "Celia, loyal and true," I managed.

She ran a strand of my hair through her fingers the way Maggie had done. "Stay alive."

I couldn't answer. I couldn't even speak.

She ducked out the door. She grabbed Patch up from the step, hugged him, then took Granda's hand. She turned one last time. "Someday . . ."

I knew she was thinking of Smith Street, Brooklyn, and all of us together. Except that she didn't know they would be there and I would be here. I could never leave Anna. I owed it to her to stay.

We stood there and waved, Patch and I; then it fell to me to wrap Biddy, limp and quiet, in a bag, and to tie a rope around Muc's neck.

Muc. How we had counted on her piglets! I remembered when Da had brought her home. "One day," he had said, eyes crinkling, "we'll have piglets for the rent. With turf in the hearth, potatoes in the pit, and a thatch on the roof, we'll need nothing more to keep us happy."

"Unless it's a bit of soil that belongs to us," Granda had said sharply. "A land that's free of the English."

I shook my head, then left Patch with Anna and took the road to the harbor. I wasn't alone. A long line of people were leading animals. Mrs. Mallon with two goats, someone with a pony and three or four pigs.

I thought about singing. I even opened my

mouth, but my throat was dry and not a sound came out. Instead I just walked with the others. All of us were quiet; only the animals made sounds.

One of Devlin's men rattled by on a cart with a few pieces of furniture: a wooden chair, a settle, a pile of rusty tools.

At the dock in the noise and the rain, I saw Anna's cow and her pig, and men whipping animals onto planks of wood that led to a ship. It was a ship filled with food that was going away from us forever.

And then I hurried home to smoor the fire. Patch and I went to bed without food, to think about Brooklyn, New York, and Celia and Granda out on the road to Galway.

# Chapter 17

Which was worse? Being alone in the dark house with Patch, or having nothing to eat but warm water with a few leaves floating around on top? No mussels were left, no limpets, no dulse. Strangers had come to the sea and taken everything, and now even they were gone.

I sat at the hearth that night, glad that Da had left us with enough turf to burn until he came back. I closed my eyes, missing him so much I had a pain in my chest. For a moment I saw him under the waves. I sat up straight. I couldn't think about that. And then I saw it, poking out of a basket. My knitting. Better yet, Celia's. Two shawls. Mine was *fuafar,* but the other was lovely. "Great girl, *a stór,* Celia," I whispered.

Patch looked up from his wall of stones. "Are you saying your prayers, Nory?"

I smiled at him. "No, talking to my own self." I patted the floor next to me and he scooted over, skinny as a strand of the wool.

"Do you remember potatoes?" He had the sound of an old man.

I gave him a hug. "I'll knit these shawls as fast as I can, and we will take them to

Ballilee straightaway and sell them."

"For coins?" Patch asked dreamily.

"Yes," I said, "and we will turn those coins into food. What do you think of that?"

I turned Celia's shawl right side out, then wrong side out. I fiddled with the needles. Knit next? Purl? Do something about fringe? I sat there with the knitting in my lap, staring first at the wool, the color of oats, and then at the turf in the hearth, bits of glowing orange blocks. My legs were heavy and my arms weak. It was hard to think.

Patch shook me. "Don't sleep, Nory."

I jumped. The fire was low now, and outside it was dark. I sat absolutely still, trying to listen to the creakings that might mean footsteps. The *sidhe*. Or strangers looking for food, looking for turf, ready to take them from me.

On my lap was food, a shawl to be turned into coins, turned into a loaf of bread, if I could just think about how to do it. I took a breath. "We will go to Anna's," I said, "and show her the shawl and she'll tell me how to finish it."

"And she will give us milk," Patch said.

I shook my head. "No. The cow is gone. Gone with Muc and Biddy to England. They will be English animals now, not Irish."

116

I thought about leaving Patch there in the house alone. I wondered if he was too weak to walk across the double field to Anna's. But I could see him falling asleep, leaning forward, and tumbling into the fire.

Not only that, I was afraid to go alone.

The wet grass squeaked under our feet. I closed the door carefully so no traveler would think it was empty, and took Patch's hand in mine. I knew the *sidhe* searched for boys to drag down into their rings. But Patch's skirt was long enough to dip along the ground, and his hair covered his ears. No one could guess he was a boy.

I stood in front of the closed door and peered across the yard and at the road. I looked everywhere to be sure no one was out there. "Come on now," I said. "We are safe."

The Mallons' house was a black smudge in the fog, the stone walls sleeping, the worn path quiet as we tiptoed over it. We ran the last few feet, breathless. I raised my hand to knock at Anna's door, but before I touched the wood, the door opened, and we rushed inside.

Anna looked pale and sick, but her voice was strong. "It is late for a visit," she said.

I held up the knitting. "I don't know how to finish this."

She took the shawl from me and put it on the table. I was so glad to be there, so glad Patch and I weren't alone, that I sank down on the floor in front of her hearth.

Anna swung the kettle over the fire, and when the water bubbled up she threw in a handful of dried herbs.

Patch was asleep in an instant, fallen across the straw in the corner. Anna covered him with a rusty black coat and came back to the fire to give me a cup of the water and to pour one for herself.

I sipped at the bitter drink, telling myself not to think about the trip back to my own dark house, or the mist outside, or the *sidhe* hiding in the hedges to grab at our feet.

Instead I watched Anna take the bundled-up knitting from the table. As I took the last sip, she moved closer to the fire and began to knit. She picked at the wool, patted it, dug the needles into it, and then her fingers were flying, the yarn moving up and over one needle and across to the other.

Patch's breath was soft and even in his corner. I breathed with him, thinking of Maggie and Da, of Celia and Granda out on the road, and of Sean Red. Where was he sleeping? Was he lying on the side of the road near the bay, freezing this night, or had he made it back to his house? I shivered.

And then I thought of Anna's son, Tague. If it had been daytime with the door open and the light coming in I would never have asked. But inside we were close together, and warm, with the fire throwing great shadows on the stone walls. The only sounds were the *click-click* of the needles and Patch's breath, and I blurted out, "Tell me about Tague."

The needles clicked for another moment. Then she began to talk. "He was always singing, never still. And after he was gone the whole world seemed quiet. I thought there'd never be another like him."

I swallowed my tea.

"But then," she said, "years later, I began to watch someone, a small child backed up against a wall, her mother dying, and there was nothing I could do." She held out her hands. "Nothing I knew would save that young mother."

I made a sound. Mam. Of course, she would have tried to save Mam. How could I have thought otherwise?

Anna nodded. "This child had such love in her, a laughing child, brave like my son. She sang. She climbed over walls. She left gates open. She danced through the cemetery and over the cliffs."

Anna ran her old hands over the shawl in

her lap. "And I loved her for that. Loved her always."

Me. She was talking about me.

"But there was more," Anna said. "I had spent a lifetime learning about plants and what they could do to heal." She bent her head. "I had to teach all this to someone. I knew that the girl who sang, the little girl who could remember the words and the songs, would remember the herbs and the magic of them."

She looked up and I could see the tears in those faded blue eyes. "But she was afraid," Anna said. "Afraid of my magic, afraid of me."

I pressed my knuckles against my mouth. "Oh, Anna," I said.

She reached forward, grasping my hand. "My coin didn't matter. I'm an old woman and it doesn't make any difference if I die, as long as I pass that healing on to you."

I wiped the tears that dripped down my own cheeks. I was bursting with love for her. I reached out to pull her close to me and leaned my head against her cap.

# Chapter 18

I dreamed of an apple, a shiny green one. The sweetness of it was in my mouth and the juice ran down my chin. I opened my eyes. Patch and I lay in a tangle of old coats with bits of straw covering us. Anna stood next to the bed with an apple in her hand.

*Still a dream,* I thought.

But this apple wasn't shiny green; it was wrinkled and almost as gray as the cloth that was tucked up under my chin.

An apple.

"Where did you get that?" I leaned up on one elbow, but Patch reached across me. Anna was almost smiling. "I saved it." She put it in his hand.

We sat on the edge of her bed, Patch and I, taking turns. I held it out to Anna once, and then a second time, but she shook her head and motioned for us to eat. We ate until it was finished, core gone, seeds gone, everything gone, even the stem. And Anna watched, nodding.

We lay back against the straw, wishing for something else to put into our mouths, wishing for another apple. Patch began to whimper. I put my hand on his arm to stop him from saying what I wanted to say myself.

He said it anyway. "Do you have another apple, Anna, please?"

She touched his soft hair. "I finished the shawl during the night," she said. "The wool is good, and the stitches are fine and even."

"Oh, Anna," I said, and swung my legs out of the straw. "I will go to Ballilee with it to sell." I sat on the edge for a moment. It was a long walk and I felt shaky even after the apple.

Patch struggled up out of the straw. "I will go with you, Nory."

Anna grabbed my wrist. "Be careful," she said sharply. "Don't let strangers see you with any money. Spend it wisely. Buy only what's necessary." She looked angrier than I had ever seen her. But I knew it wasn't anger. The lines and furrows in her face had to do with worry.

"I will be careful," I said. "I will buy what we need and then come back. Will you . . ."

". . . take care of the little one," she said.

I nodded.

"No." Patch began to cry. "We will buy a penny bun."

I swooped down to give him a hug, but I didn't stop to tell him he couldn't go with me. I just went, listening to his crying.

It was a beautiful day, the sea laid out flat

and gray, and in back of me the sun coming up over the cliffs. I walked slowly, the shawl hidden under my petticoat. But no one was on the path this morning. Scavengers were at the water's edge where nothing would wash up. The land was bare as well. Even the grass was sparse because people had pulled up huge clumps to suck on. Nothing else grew, except the razor-sharp sea grass on the sand dunes near the water.

I kept walking, planning. How much would I get for the shawl? Whom would I sell it to? What was the most important thing to buy afterward? And I thought of the package in the post office.

I reached the main street at last. People filled the street, people with no money for a shawl, no money for food. They stood in front of the bakery, waiting, coughing, holding each other up. Others were at the hotel, hands out, swaying a little. Their eyes were huge in their bony faces. And even though the day was cold, some of them wore almost no clothing, just pieces of rags. One woman had only her petticoat. *They must have sold whatever they could,* I thought, *to buy a bit of food.*

I pushed through them to the door of the hotel, and I waited too, looking through the lobby window.

Inside, women were sitting in front of the hearth. One of them wore a ribboned hat that dipped and bobbed as she spoke. A woman with a brooch and rings sparkling as she moved. Lord Cunningham's wife!

She was holding a thick piece of brack to her mouth. But a man guarded the doors; he was so big I'd never be able to pass him. I held up the shawl so the people around me couldn't see it, but I hoped the woman in the hat did.

I stood there for a long time watching her take delicate bites of the brack, wondering how it must be to have so much food. At last she wiped her buttery fingers on a piece of cloth and turned toward me. She looked at the shawl, then motioned to the guard.

He opened the door just enough to take the shawl for her. The woman held it up, feeling the ribs of it, running one finger over the pattern. The hat bobbed once again. She reached into a small red purse and gave coins to the guard.

I saw him put one in his pocket before he opened the door, but he dropped three others into the palm of my hand.

I took the steps down from the hotel, pushing my way between two women with babies, and the children who were sitting in the street. I darted around the side of the hotel and sank down in a quiet spot. The coins were of different sizes; how much were they were worth?

I thought about bread, or a handful of oats. But most of all I thought about the package that lay on the shelf in the post office. If I could have it in my hands, it would be better than a loaf of bread. It would be like having Maggie back with us in Maidin Bay.

But Patch needed food more than a package that might be anything, or almost nothing. What would Maggie do?

I stood up at last, feeling dizzy, hungrier than I had ever been, and started up the street, walking around the groups of people. I had never seen so many before. Some of them lay against the walls of the shops, looking as if they'd never get up, their eyes sunken in their heads. They were almost like skeletons. And it was quiet now, so quiet. I pulled my shawl over my mouth and made my way around them to the post office.

The window was filthy. I peered through the dirt at the shelf with the box and its bits of colored paper, and the *R* for *Ryan*. But Patch's face was in my mind, and Anna's. Suppose there was no food in that box or nothing that could be turned into food? But there was something inside that Maggie thought we wanted or needed. What?

I leaned against a piece of glass in the window to stop the pounding in my head. It was cool and I hated to move. But I went through the alley to the back of the bakery with the coins tight in my hands.

At the doorway, I held out one of the coins the way I had held out the shawl, covering it so only the baker could see what I was holding. After a while he came to the door and reached for the coin with his dusty white hands. He came back with a knob of flour in a twist of paper and a handful of oats in a small bag.

What else could I buy? I hurried, head down, to the main street again with the package under my shawl. I had to find something that would last.

A man holding a can blocked my way. "It's milk," he said, "the last from my cow before they took her away." He bit his lips, chapped as Celia's and mine were, but there was something about him, his eyes almost hidden under straggly hair, that made me think of Devlin. I took a step away.

He followed me. "The whole can for a coin."

My headache was worse; I was dizzy, trying to think of what to do.

Should I buy it?

Would I spill the milk on the way home?

It had a strange color after all, almost like one of Biddy's eggs. I shook my head and took another step and another . . .

. . . and backed into the doorway of the post office.

I was dizzy, thinking of Maggie's face in front of me. She shook her head, *no,* and Celia said, *"You never think of what you're doing."*

I should put this coin into Anna's hand. Instead I put a coin on the counter. I couldn't even speak. I just pointed up. Somehow I knew Anna wouldn't mind.

The postman looked down at the coin. He shook his head, so I put down the last coin. And then the package was in front of me, and I was putting my *N* on a lined piece of paper. "To say that you received it, you know," he said.

I went out the door, holding it, weighing it in my mind, not heavy, not light. I ran my fingers over the bits of color, red and green, and the writing. I could even pick out my own *N,* and Celia's *C,* as well as the *R* for our *Ryan.* But I didn't stop to open it. I took the narrow twisting road that circled Maidin Bay and led toward home. Through my dizziness I could still see us, the three of us, around Anna's hearth. We'd have a dollop of stirabout each and enough flour for a tiny loaf of bread that would last us for days. And maybe by that time Celia and Granda would be back, and Da with coins in his pocket, and I would tell him, "Anna first."

As I reached the top of the hill, I saw her house below. My head was full of my packages and how I would put them on the table and what Anna would say and what Patch would do. I hardly felt the rain as it pelted down on me, covering the road and the rock walls on each side. I hardly noticed the fog as it blotted out the cliffs.

By the time I heard the footsteps it was too late. I felt a hand on the back of my neck, felt the push. I threw my hands out to stop myself from falling, but it didn't help. There was a sudden pain as I went down and a rock tore open my forehead.

I looked up to see the man running with my packages under his arm, his hair streaming out in back of him. His can of milk rolled down the hill, splashing milk as it went.

I closed my eyes. I didn't want to see anything else. Celia was right. *I didn't think.*

It seemed as if my eyes were closed for only a minute, even though it was dark when I opened them and I lay in the straw of

Anna's bed, shivering. Anna and Patch crouched on the floor next to me, both watching.

Anna held up my head and poured something into my mouth. Something bitter, *fuafar*. And even though I could hardly think, I knew the herb: comfrey.

"Nory is sick," Patch said, but Anna shook her head. "Not sick, shocked. Something happened to her."

The sound of a cloth being ripped, cool water on my head, the smell of comfrey. I was asleep, and then awake, listening to Patch ask for food, to Anna as she made a soup for him and tucked him in beside me, still listening as Patch's breath slowed and thickened in sleep.

Anna's hand was on my cheek. "It's all right," she kept saying. "It will be all right."

I opened my eyes once, and then, at last, I really slept.

# Chapter 19

How long had I slept? Was it hours or days? For the first time I wasn't hungry. I wasn't cold, either. It was as if I'd been leaning against the sunwarmed rocks at Patrick's Well in June. Deep in the straw I could feel the roundness of Patch's heel against my back.

But there was something I had to think about. What was it? I turned, just the smallest bit, but it was enough to lose the warm spot I had made. I folded my arms over my chest and curved my back, digging my chin down, folding myself into a ball.

The thing to think about: maybe it was just a sneeze coming. I wiggled my nose, but the straw was old, settled. It wasn't that. I had a quick picture of Da standing outside our doorway one summer, the rick of hay caught on the edge of his pitchfork. "New bedding," he said, and the dust of the hay had swirled in the sunlight like a shower of gold. *Ah, Da.*

It came back to me, as Patch moved again, whimpered. I had lost everything. Patch was going to die, and Anna. We were all going to die, the three of us, here in the straw, warm and cozy, but without food.

And then the other thing. The thing I'd been pressing out of my head. The cliffs. The sound of them, almost as if they were alive, screaming in the wind, and far below, the pounding of the surf with the spray shooting high into the air, and falling back and back, taking bits of rock and stone, and anyone who was clinging there.

Pale light came in under the door. We'd slept half the morning away. I reached out, and Patch moved closer in his sleep. Could Anna be asleep too?

Up on my elbow, I peered across the room at the other straw bed. If I had seen her that way last year I would have been sure she was a witch: wisps of white hair, wrinkled cheeks, long fingers clutching the coats that covered her.

I rolled out of the bed, my head throbbing, and felt her eyes on me. I went first to the hearth to blow the fire into life. Then I leaned over her. "Are you sick?"

She shook her head, but I wasn't satisfied. "Do you have something to eat in the house?" I asked. "Is there anything for you at all?" But I knew the answer before she told me. The coin, the milk, the apple. I had taken them all.

"My fault," I said.

131

She shook her head and said something to me, but she was mumbling. I caught the word *song* and then *Tague*. She reached up and patted my sleeve. Then she was quiet again, sleeping.

I looked back at Patch. There was nothing to him but a small fold under the clothes. The hand against his cheek was nothing but bones.

We had to have something to eat. Something more than water with roots and leaves Anna had saved. We had to have real food.

Anna spoke without opening her eyes. "They are starving to death in their houses," she said.

"Yes," I told her, a tap of pain in my forehead.

"We would have had enough," she said, "even without the potatoes, if the English had left us the animals, the grain."

I thought of Biddy and her sisters laying warm brown eggs in their baskets, Muc to have piglets one day. All gone down to the harbor and across the sea to the English.

Only the birds that flew over the cliffs in Maidin Bay were left.

I swallowed. It was there again. A picture of the cliffs, great monsters with the wind screaming, tearing.

I sat back on my heels, thinking I couldn't

do it, that no one could do it. But I heard Maggie saying, *You will know what to do yourself. Great girl, a stór.*

"I know a way to get food." I reached out to touch Anna's forehead. She had a fever. I went to the table and mixed the greens together, stirring as I watched her. A moment later I put my arm under her, lifted her, and made her drink. A sip, two sips. I hoped it would be enough.

I boiled water next, and put a handful of herbs to float in it for a soup. I raised Patch's head to give him some, then left the rest of it on the floor next to him. "I will be gone a long time," I told him, "and you will stay here." I bit my lip. "Stay right in this warm bed."

Outside I picked up two stones, one triangular and one perfectly round. I went back inside and left them for Patch to find next to the soup; then I wrapped my shawl around my shoulders and went across the field, thinking of Celia and Granda, wondering if they were alive. When I reached the Mallons' house, I stopped. It was almost a miracle. Sean Red was huddled outside on the step in the pale sun. His head was down, but he looked up as I called, *"Dia duit."* He smiled when he saw who it was.

I sat beside him, looking at his face.

133

Something had happened to his teeth. They looked huge in his face. And then I saw that his teeth weren't different but his face had changed. His cheeks were sunken and flat like Granda's; his eyes were deep in his head. He looked at me and I knew he was thinking I looked terrible too.

"Oh, Sean," I said. We moved closer, leaning against each other.

"I know where there is food," I said slowly, the way I had to Anna. "Enough to keep us going. Maybe all of us. Your mother and Granny . . ."

"Granny's gone." He raised one hand toward the cemetery.

I shook my head. "But we didn't pray over her."

No wake, no funeral. And then I thought about it. No money for the food and the *poitín* at the wake. And who was left to come? People were trying to get a ship to America, or they were sick lying in the streets of Ballilee, or just wandering out on the road as Devlin put them out of their houses.

Sean looked as if he didn't have the strength of Patch, but I couldn't think of that now. "How are your hands, Sean Red?" I asked. "Are they strong enough to hold me on a line?"

His head was down again, his hands dangling.

"I am going out on the cliffs," I said. "Like Tague. I'll take the eggs of the wild birds if I can find them."

Still he didn't answer. But wasn't that like Sean, hating to open his mouth? I began again. "Do you think I like to talk to the top of your red head?" I tapped his shoulder. "It's not your head I need, it's your hands."

He put out his hands and showed me the palms: red and purple, bruised, cut, and blistered. He couldn't even bend his fingers.

I bit my lip so hard I could taste the blood. He'd never hold a rope; he couldn't hold anything.

"They wouldn't let me work on the road anymore," he said.

I knew what that meant. The Mallons had no way of getting food.

I grabbed his sleeve, feeling the long bones of his arm underneath. "We will find a way," I said. "We'll have food for you and your mother, for Anna, and Patch, and we'll hold ourselves over until we plant again, or until my da comes back."

"And someday we will go to Brooklyn, New York, America," Sean said.

"Smith Street," I whispered.

In my head I saw the box with its bits of

colored paper and the *R* that stood for *Ryan.*

"You can't go down on a rope," he said. "Tague was killed that way. You know that."

"Do you think I'm going to die for want of food," I asked, "when it's there on the cliffs waiting for me?" But even as I said it I wondered if I could do it. I looked up across the fields. I could almost see Da there, and Celia and Granda, coming to save us.

# Chapter 20

"We can't," Sean said again.

"Will you say this all afternoon?" I asked him. "Until the sun falls away from us and the birds go back to their nests?"

He made a sound, but I didn't listen. "First we'll get the ropes," I said. "Then we'll go up to the cliff."

"I will never hold you," he said, putting his hands up to his face. "But you could hold me."

"And how would you carry the eggs without breaking them?" I tried to smile.

He nodded. "We'll tie the rope to my waist then and to the rocks. If we cover my hands with cloth, I will manage somehow, Nory." He looked into my face. "I will never let you fall."

"I know that, Sean Red."

He looked back at the door of his house, a quiet house without the sound of his mother's scolding. Was she lying in her bed, as sick as Anna?

I looked across the field. A small shape tottered toward me. I stood up. "Patch."

"I'm coming, Nory," he called. "Coming to find you."

My hand went to my mouth. What could I do with him?

"We can't take him," Sean said.

I shook my head. There was no time to go back to Anna's. And there was only silence in Mallons' house. "We can't leave him."

"He'll fall."

I ran my tongue over my dry lips. "We'll lash him to a rock. We'll make sure he doesn't fall. Somehow we'll do that."

He sighed. "Yes, all right." He walked away from me then, going around the side of the house for his brothers' fishing ropes, reaching for the cart to carry them, using his wrists rather than his hands.

He leaned into the cart, pushing it with his body, and stopped at the end of the yard so I could find a place for Patch on top of the ropes, a place so small that his feet grazed the ground. "I'll pull it," I said.

The climb was almost a dream, the rocky road under my feet, the road rising. The wind was just a breath at first, and then it tore at my face. There was a blast of it as we reached the top. *I am Maeve,* I thought, remembering the day I had twirled over the rocks singing, with nothing to worry about, with Maggie still home and the potatoes growing green in the field.

We sat near the well and rested, watching

the birds soar over us, screaming back and forth to each other. Then it was time. I stood up, bent because of the wind, shivering, listening to Patch crying. "Cold, Nory, cold, cold."

I went back and put my face against his, my arms around him. "You will build great stone walls someday." I fluttered my eyelashes against his cheeks, rubbed his back. "Soon we will go back to Anna's. I will cook you an egg, two eggs, Patcheen with the blue stone eyes."

I reached under him with my arms and tugged him out of the cart as Sean began to uncoil the rope, using his arms, butting his head under it so it looped around his neck.

"It will be warmer back among the rocks," I told Patch, "out of the wind."

Patch shook his head. "Not there." Someone had told him about the gray smoke men who lived in the rocks, I knew that.

I put my hands on his cold little cheeks and tried to think of what I could tell him. And then I said in my loudest, fiercest voice, "No gray smoke men will dare. No *sidhe*, no *bean sidhe*. I am Nora Ryan and I come from Queen Maeve and Mam and Granda and Da. And you, Patrick Ryan, are safe with me."

And then I saw Sean Red and stuck my chin out so he'd know too that I meant what I said.

I turned back to Patch. "I'll take a bit of rope, twirl it around you." I tried to make it sound like a game. "You'll be warm, Patcheen, you'll dream of building a wall with blue stones."

He was crying again, tears from the blue stone eyes.

I kept moving with him, trying to find a space to wedge him in. The place I found was almost a bowl, rocks curved up and around with just enough room for one wee man, I thought, or one small boy. But after I had wedged him in, I knew there was no way to tie him. Too loose and he'd slip out, too tight and he wouldn't be able to move.

"You have to stay here, Patcheen, stay still, don't move. It's a place to fall. Will you stay?"

Sean was calling me now. "Hurry."

I could see the shadows falling across the cliffs. My legs ached, and my arms. It was hard to think. "Sleep," I told Patch. "I'll be back, back in a moment, back in a while."

I slipped down off the rocks, onto the bare ground of the cliff where Sean was waiting, the rope curled around his shoulder.

"Listen, Nory," he said. "You have to turn

into the rope as the wind spins you. Test each rock with your foot before you rest on it. You have to be quiet, be quick, and watch your face, your eyes. The birds will fight to save their nests."

I put up my hand. I didn't want to hear any more.

"There's a ledge," he said. "I don't know how far down. But we've seen it from the shore. There are chinks and cracks and messy nests."

"With eggs," I said, reaching for his cap. "I'll fill this, you'll see. But we have to hurry." My lips chattered. "Patcheen will be up."

"I'll watch him," he said, but I knew he'd be holding the rope, watching me. If Patch wandered onto the edge . . .

*Stop,* I told myself, and in my mind, *Celia.*

I couldn't think about that. Instead I'd think of the eggs round and warm in my hands. I'd think of opening them, one for me and one for Patch. Think of spooning a warm egg soup into Anna's mouth. Think of Sean.

Sean kept talking as we sat ourselves on the ground and wound the rope around our waists, wound ourselves together. His face tightened as the rope touched his hands.

It was beginning to rain, a soft slanting

rain that went through my shawl. We stood up and danced away from each other, pulling on the rope at our waists, to be sure it was tight. I pointed. "I'll go down that way."

"*A brave child like my son,*" Anna had said. *Please let me be brave.*

"Don't face the sea, face the rocks," Sean said. "Don't look down."

I watched him wedge himself in, his feet up, his hands wrapped in a cloth holding the rope. "I'll hold my own weight," I said, "you know that." I didn't say what we were both thinking. If I lost my footing and fell, he'd have to depend on the strength of his body and the rocks to keep me from going into the sea. He'd never be able to use his hands.

"If you're in trouble," he said, "the rope will tighten against me. Otherwise it will be slow and steady, and you will give a tug on it once in a while so I know you are still . . ."

"Alive." I tried to grin at him. "Bringing you an egg for your breakfast."

"Two eggs." He tried to smile. "There is a hole in my stomach where there should be food."

I touched his hand, made the sign of the cross over myself . . .

And took a step.

And another.

And turned my back away from the sea.

And lowered myself down, one rock at a time, feeling with my toes, testing each rock as Sean had said, to make sure it would hold me.

And rested, catching my breath, leaning my head against a slab of a rock, my feet on a wide flag.

And listened with my eyes closed to the sound of the wind and the surf and the spray crashing against the cliff below. *Don't look at the sea,* but I had to look over my shoulder, a quick look, the quickest look.

The clouds drifted across the sea and away again, making patterns of light on the water in the distance, and suddenly the sound of what I was hearing, the whistle of the wind across the cliffs, the booming of the surf, was music. And at that moment I felt like Queen Maeve.

I felt Sean tugging at the rope. He must have wondered why I had stopped. I tugged back with my free hand to let him know I was all right.

From there it was not as hard. I made music in my own mind to go with the music of the cliffs. And my hands held each rock above and my feet found the right places one after another . . .

Until I reached down and there was no

rock under me. I circled the air with my leg, toes pointed, searching for something, a rock, a ledge. Suddenly there was a screaming in my ears and a great flapping of wings against my head and in my hair. Claws raked my forehead, opening a cut. Blood ran over my eye and down my cheek, and I screamed with the same sound as the bird.

Without thinking, I let go of the rock to beat it away. I dropped, one hand still holding the bird's legs, feeling the dizziness as the sea below tilted and moved up toward me. With a sickening crunch I landed on the ledge.

The screeching of the bird stopped and I saw that it was dead under me. I moved as far away from it as I could on the edge, so far that my back was up against the wall of rock. I could feel Sean pulling on the rope. I tugged again and lay there, thinking I'd never get up, never get away from the bird.

I saw the nests above me, within my reach, and got up on my knees, shouting, waving my arms, to be sure there wasn't a bird on a nest that would startle me into falling again.

The birds wheeled above me, screeching, their powerful wings flapping. I took the eggs quickly, searching out the largest ones, putting them carefully in Sean's cap, nesting them in bits of grass to be sure they wouldn't break. I left an egg in each nest.

And then I was finished. There was more to eat in that cap than we'd had in days. I pictured the eggs bubbling gently in the boiling water, tried to think how long they'd last, because I'd have to do this again, and again, until Da came back, or Celia and Granda.

I crawled back along the ledge, trying not to look at the poor dead bird, its feathers blowing in the wind.

The bird. What would Celia think of me if I left it there? A giant of a bird, more than one meal.

I reached out and touched it. *Fuafar*. And then I tied it to my waist and began to climb back up the cliff.

# Chapter 21

Every day was a day to get through, a day to wonder about Celia and Granda, a day to long for Da. Anna watched me, shaking her head. She was stronger now, and one morning at last she left her bed and went slowly to the doorway. She looked toward the cliffs. I knew she was looking for Maeve. "It is all I need," she said, nodding at me. "A dog at my hearth, a few weeds for medicine, and a field of growing potatoes."

I felt a quick pain in my chest. I knew where Maeve was. I opened my mouth, wondering what to say, but then I saw Sean and his cart coming down the road toward us.

Sean was stronger too. I had climbed down the cliff again and again. We had cooked birds, tasting horribly of the sea, eaten their eggs, and Sean had dipped his hands into the bay every day until they began to heal.

It wasn't that we weren't hungry. We were hungry all the time. And Patch was still thin, still white, his skirt big enough for two boys his size.

I went outside to take a breath of the

damp air and there was Sean, coming down the road, waving, and his mother lumped up on the edge of the cart, holding a small chest on her lap. "We are leaving," she called. "Leaving for Galway to find a ship."

Sean leaving? Not Sean, too! My fist went to my mouth, hard against my teeth. We had always been together, the two of us.

He reached out and took my hand from my mouth. "A friend of Liam's," he said, "stopped with the papers last night. He told us that Liam and Michael had worked on the docks before they sailed to America."

"And what of Da and Celia and . . ."

Before I could finish, he shook his head. "There are so many people at the dock." He reached for my other hand. "There is one extra ticket, Nory. Granny's ticket. And it is for you."

*Smith Street, Brooklyn. Horses clopping down the streets. Maggie waiting at the door. Food.*

"Come with me, Nory," he said.

Anna spoke from the doorway. "I will keep Patch for you. He will be safe with me."

But even as she said it, I shook my head. I would never leave her. It was Patch who had to go to America, Patch who had to have that chance. "Will you, Sean Red . . . ," I began, and he knew what I was going to say.

147

Mrs. Mallon knew too. "How can we take someone so small?" she asked, but Sean held up his hand.

We looked at each other, the two of us, and I remembered walking to Patrick's Well together. How many times? I had danced with him at Maggie's wedding, making faces at Celia. *Dear Celia.* I remembered singing and sharing dulse with him. I remembered the cliffs.

Sean nodded. "You can trust him with me."

"Don't I know that?" I told myself I couldn't cry now, not until they were gone. I went to the side of Anna's house. Patch was there, bent over, humming to himself, piling one stone on top of another. I sat down next to him and touched his hair and his little shoulders, and his neck that was almost too thin to hold up his head. "Someone is waiting for you," I said.

He looked up at me with blue stone eyes. "And who is that, Nory?"

I could hardly talk. "It is your own Maggie," I said. "You will climb up on the cart with Mrs. Mallon. You will take your best stones and your coat. And a ship will be waiting for you in Galway."

"The *Emma Pearl*," he said dreamily. "And you, too, on the cart."

I shook my head. "I must stay here. I will find stones for you and send them someday."

He shook his head, beginning to sob, reaching out for me. I held him, his hair fine under my hands, his arms tight around me. He was the last one left.

I pried his fingers away. "You must go," I said, my voice hard. "Maggie is waiting, and there will be food."

"No." He pulled at my arm, at my skirt. "Let me stay."

"Maggie will be waiting at the port of New York for you. She will lift you up, hug you. She will be so happy to see you."

He was on the ground now, sobbing, his face buried in the earth. I pulled him up on his knees, looking into that little face. "You will find stones in America. You will build a house and tall buildings."

He shook his head hard.

I cupped his cheeks in my hands, kissed his tiny nose. "You will remember something, when you are an old man like Granda." I said it slowly, each word above the noise of his crying. "You will say that your own Nory sent you because she loved you. You will say that no one ever loved you more."

He shut his eyes over his tears, the lids swollen.

"Patcheen with the blue stone eyes," I said, and stopped. I could not cry. Not yet. I darted into the house, trying to think. An egg hard-boiled for one pocket, another for his hand, a pile of stones. And Anna grabbed up the old black coat to cover him.

I went out to the cart, looking at Sean, looking at Mrs. Mallon. "You will put him into Maggie's hands, then," I said.

"It is where we are going, after all," Mrs. Mallon said in her harsh voice, but moving over, making room for him on the edge of the cart.

I bent over him and pulled him up, his legs kicking out, and his arms. "No, Nory, no," he cried as Sean took him from me and put him up on the cart.

Sean turned back to me. "I will see you on Smith Street," he said. "We will climb cliffs if they are there to be climbed."

I reached out to touch his forehead. *"Dia duit."* Then I stepped back and Sean began to pull the cart.

"Remember," I called to Sean. "Remember me." I waved to them all the way down the road, even though I could hardly see for the tears. I could hear Patch crying for me a little longer. Then they were gone. I stood there, my forehead against the wall of Anna's house, feeling its roughness against my skin, sobbing, as Anna rested her hands on my shoulders.

At last I turned to her. "Gone," I said. "All of them."

She gripped her clay pipe in her mouth. "I don't know why life is so hard," she said. "But I do know this, Nory Ryan. It is a lucky house to have you in it."

I wiped my eyes with my sleeve and the back of my hand. "I will walk up to my house. I will see what food there is to find." We both knew there was nothing there. But I couldn't stay there for another minute. I needed time to take deep breaths, time to walk along the road by myself. Later in the day I'd go down the side of the cliff for eggs again. I didn't need Sean Red. I had gouged out small pieces of rocks, places to fit my feet. I knew where to hold, where to lean, where to rest.

I walked to my own house first, added a piece of turf to the fire, ran my hands over the stones in the hearth. I knew the house would be tumbled any day now, but I'd never let the fire go out until then.

A trail of stones wandered along the floor. *Patch.* I caught my breath.

I looked out the door the way Anna had, still searching for Da every day, even though I was sure now he'd never come. And then I took the steps over the stile and went through the old cemetery. I stopped for a prayer at St. Erna's shrine, leaning under the roof to stay out of the wind. I remembered the stones piled up around the statue, Da fitting each one perfectly together; remembered his smile as he touched the statue's feet: *"It'll keep the old monk out of the rain for another hundred years or so."*

Something was caught against the stone wall. What was it? A piece of wood? I reached for it, and as I pulled it out gently, I could see it was a piece of a box.

A piece of our box! The box that had come all the way from Smith Street. The man must have pried it open and left the part that didn't matter. But it did matter. It made all the difference. I sat back on my heels, holding it against my chest. *Maggie had touched it too.* I turned it over, patting the rough piece of wood, and it was even more wonderful than I had thought. It had been sheltered from the wind and the rain in back of the shrine, so I could still see what Maggie had drawn.

This picture was different from her usual ones, drawn with thin lines of color, greens and yellows, instead of thick peat lines. I could see a row of houses stuck together, and in front were people, stretched along that Smith Street, and I knew who they were.

Da was there, the tallest, and Granda next to him, and Patch on one end, looking up. Celia and I were in the middle, making faces at each other, and Francey had one arm around Maggie.

And Maggie! She had made a small curve in her long skirt so it billowed out, and one hand was over her waist. I ran my fingers over Maggie and her full skirt, so glad the man who had stolen the package never knew he had left the best for me.

Staying there in Maidin Bay wasn't going to be the worst thing. I would have Anna, and I knew by the small *N* Maggie had drawn over her skirt that there was going to be a baby, and she meant to name her Nory.

I stood up then and told myself for the hundredth time that year that I would never cry again. Then I saw someone coming. Devlin! And when he saw me he reined in his horse. "You," he called. "It's you I want to see."

# Chapter 22

"You are staying with Anna Donnelly." He tilted his head toward Anna's house.

I didn't answer. I tucked my hands under my shawl, clenching my fingers.

But he showed his long teeth in a smile. "The landlord is here for a visit. He needs healing." He waved his hand. "I thought I'd talk to you about it instead of the old woman."

I stared at the horse, at Devlin's rough boots, then up at his face. And standing in the road, I knew I could do something for Anna at last. It was hard to get out the words. "Sometimes she heals," I said, "and sometimes she doesn't." I made myself raise one shoulder just the slightest bit.

"I remember she does something about stomach pains." He ran his hand over his waist.

I had to tell Anna. He hadn't forgotten about that cure after all.

"Broken bones," said Devlin. "And wens."

"And the fever people are having in Ballilee," I said, taking a guess about what might be wrong with the landlord.

I saw the light come into his eyes, but I

shook my head before he could say anything. "Anna is not healing now." My mouth was dry. "Her dog is missing, a black-and-white dog with a freckled muzzle."

He narrowed his eyes, staring at me.

"She needs the dog."

Devlin looked back and up at the land-lord's house. "I will send the dog."

I closed my eyes. "Food."

"There is little food in the whole land."

"It has gone to England," I said bitterly. "But someday the potatoes will grow again. She will need the seed potatoes and help planting them."

"All right."

"I will ask her." I stopped and started again. "As soon as she has the dog and food. Just a little food. She doesn't need much."

"Don't go too far," he said, but nodded just the slightest bit.

I clutched the rough wood of Maggie's box to my chest. Before I could answer, he rode away. I waited until he was gone, and then I ran across the fields to Anna's door.

We laid the piece of the box on the table with Anna's cures and made ourselves a bit of hot water to sip while I told her all that had happened, almost all. I kept the part about Maeve to myself. Suppose Devlin changed his mind?

155

"There will be food for you," I told her, "and seeds to plant when the *sidhe* are finished deviling us in the fields. And I —"

"We will share everything," she said.

I shook my head. "There won't be enough for that." I drew myself up. "I am strong, Anna. I will bring down the eggs as long as they're there, and the birds when I can. If I have to, I'll work on the roads."

I looked down at my hands, rough now but strong. I shook off the memory of Sean's hands, blistered and bleeding. Nothing would be as hard as letting Patch go.

In the dim light Anna's eyes were sparkling; I knew they were filled with tears. I took a sip of the water. It was hot enough to scald my tongue, but the heat of the cup warmed my hands as I stole a look at the drawing on the box.

How could it be that I would never see any of them again? Not Da with the smiling lines around his eyes. Not big Maggie. Not any of them. And where was Patch this night? Somewhere on the road, out in the cold.

Anna and I dozed then, heads bent forward. It was late when I heard something. Was there someone on the path? Startled, I jumped to my feet.

Anna looked up, awake now. "Nory?" she asked.

I went past her to the door to see what was out there. Then I looked back at her over my shoulder. "I think there's a bit of good to this day."

I opened the door and Maeve sailed past me, her lovely ears back, her tail high as Anna stood there, hands out, and the dog went around the table and into her arms.

I watched them for a moment, and then I ran my fingers over the wood of the box, gently over each one of my family. I went back to the hearth and swung the pot over the fire. We'd have one more cup of water to get us through the night.

# Chapter 23

The next day I went down to the sea, hoping to find something that might have washed up on shore.

"Almost anything might be turned into a little food," Anna said.

And there it was: enough kelp for a soup tumbled in on the surf.

I went back, happy to tell Anna she was right. And as we stood at the door, a man came along the cliff road. It surprised us because strangers never came this far anymore. He looked bent and worn as if every step was an effort.

He stopped when he saw us. "Ryan?" he called. "Nora Ryan?"

"Yes," I said, wondering, looking at Anna. "Who . . ."

"Come in," Anna said.

He didn't answer. He went past us and sank down on the stool at the hearth.

He was a big man, dark, his face tanned, his beard ragged. He sat with his head down and his arms between his legs, looking as if all he wanted to do was sleep.

"Your father . . . ," he said.

I stood there, hardly breathing. "Alive?" I

asked. "Is he alive?"

The answer seemed to take forever, but then he nodded. "I have a message from him. And tickets."

I backed up against the wall, feeling my legs tremble. *Alive.*

"It was a long trip we took, a second trip. There was no way to let you know. He is still working, unloading the ship."

*Alive.*

The man nodded as if even that was an effort. He reached inside his coat for two small pieces of paper, tickets like the ones Sean Red had. "Your father says you are to take the road to Galway. Stay on it and you will come to the ships. He will be waiting."

*Da's blue eyes, his hands, his face. The road is like a ball of yarn let loose. Da alive. Da waiting.*

The man pulled himself to his feet. "I must go." And when I still didn't move, didn't take the tickets from him, he put them on the table.

Anna shook her head. "Stay," she said. "Rest."

"I must go to Gweedore," he said, "and my family. I know I am needed."

He started for the door, but I took his sleeve. "Did you see a cart along the road? A little boy . . ."

159

He shook his head. "I've been so tired. I'm sorry."

"And at the docks. My sister. My grandfather."

He raised his hands, thinking. "I don't know," he said. "I just don't know."

I closed my eyes.

"It doesn't mean . . . ," Anna began, and stopped.

The man went out the door, and I realized I hadn't thanked him. I went after him to throw my arms around him. We stood there, rocking, and then he put his hand on my head. "I must go to my own children."

I watched him trudge down the road and then went into the house to stare at the tickets with Anna. Bits of paper that would take someone across the sea to the country we loved without ever having seen it. America.

Something went through my mind and was gone.

What was it?

Two tickets.

One for me? One for Anna?

"No." I said it aloud. "He would have meant one for me. One for Patch."

Anna stared at me with her faded blue eyes, and we realized, both of us, at the same moment. I clutched at her. "He would have sent tickets for all of us, for Celia, for Granda."

"Unless . . . ," Anna said.

"Unless they were there at the port. Unless he had seen them."

"Yes," Anna said.

"Alive," I said, loving the feel of the word on my tongue, the sound of it. "All of them." I looked down at her, the wisps of gray hair under the white cap. I touched the tickets. "There is one for you now, Anna."

She smiled. "I will never leave my house, my hearth, Nory Ryan. And how could I leave the *madra*? I will stay here forever."

I remembered my promise to her. I remembered all that I owed her. "I will never use my ticket either," I said. They'd be waiting; when I didn't come, they'd wonder what to do.

Anna shook her head. "There is something I want to show you. Something I have hidden from you." She reached into the basket and pulled out a shawl. It was the *fuafar* shawl I had never finished. I had to look carefully to see where I had dropped the stitches.

"I have been working on it," she said. "I always knew that someday you'd leave, and this is for you to wear on the road to Galway."

I ran my hands over it, the creamy color, the soft warmth of it.

"You will reach the harbor and a ship. If you hurry, you may catch up with Patch. You will move faster than they can."

*A ship like the* Emma Pearl. "But the ticket," I said.

She waved her hand. "You'll find someone to use it in Galway. But next winter," she said, "I will be here, warm at my hearth with Maeve. I will mix my cures" — she turned her head, looking out the door, up at the cliffs — "remembering the girl who sang like my son. A brave girl."

I put my head up, my chin out. "We belong here together."

She frowned, deep creases appearing on her forehead and around her mouth. "I belong here," she said. "But you belong in America, Nory Ryan. And you'll bring something with you. My cures. My medicine. A gift to that young free country."

*Ivy for burns, comfrey for fever, foxglove for heart pain, laurel leaves for ringworm, house-leek for the eyes, the web of a spider for bleeding.*

"Anna," I said.

She clutched my arm so hard I knew it would leave marks. "You will do this for me."

162

# Chapter 24

I went to Devlin with the bottle under my shawl. "It may work and it may not," I told him exactly as Anna had said. "Sometimes it does, and sometimes it doesn't."

Then for one last time I took the sharp little path up to Patrick's Well. I thought of Cat Neely. We'd never know what had happened to her.

A soft spring rain had begun. There were wishes to make before I left. First to wish on Anna's coin at last: *May she be warm in her house with the dog, and may the* sídhe *never cross her doorstep.*

And then on Cat Neely's yarn: *Let the ship she sailed bring her to a happy place.*

Overhead was the tree with the tiny piece of Celia's shift. Only a few colorless strings were left of it. I reached under my skirt to tear off a strip of my own petticoat and hung it next to hers. *Please let us stand in front of the house at Smith Street, every one of us, just the way Maggie drew it on the wood.*

I had to hurry now; it was getting dark. I went along the twisting path and climbed the stile that led to our field. Inside the house, I ran my hands over Maggie's drawings on the walls. I would never see the house tumbled. It would always be this way in my mind.

Under the straw was Mam's red wedding dress. I reached for it, knowing Celia and I would wear it someday. We'd eat Maggie's brack and dance. I smoothed the dress with my hands as I knelt over the small fire that had glowed in the Ryans' hearth for more than a hundred years. It took almost nothing to smother it, just a few small pats with the black potato pot. And then the house was dark.

I went back to Anna's for the last night, to share a cup of hot water and to sleep for a few hours. And then it was time to leave. A thin mist rose over the sea. Above were the cliffs, and at the very top was Patrick's Well, a dark shadow against the sky. It made me think of Sean Red. *We will be in Brooklyn together someday.*

I kissed Anna goodbye, holding her thin shoulders in my hands. "I love you, Anna Donnelly," I said.

"And I you, Nory Ryan." She wiped my face with the corner of her apron and pressed a bag of dried leaves into my hands. "I will think of you in Smith Street," she said. "I will think of you singing. I will think of you happy, and without hunger."

"The day will come," I said, "when I have money. And I will send what I have to you."

"And don't I know that?" she said.

"I'll make sure there will be nothing owing on the package." We smiled at each other, and then at last it was my turn to go up the road, as the others had, to walk backward for as long as I could see Anna at her doorway, her hand resting on Maeve's head.

"I will remember you," I called to Anna.

I followed the path to the crossroads and stopped to scoop up two stones, one white and one blue, to take with me for Patch. Then I turned to the road that wound around the coast like a ball of yarn let loose.

*416 Smith Street, Brooklyn.*

*Milk in cans, no one hungry.*

*A song.*

*All of us together. Free.*

*America.*

Dear Reader,

*An Gorta Mór* is an Irish term that stands for the Great Hunger of 1845–1852. It reminds us that many of us are Americans because of that time: the potatoes turning black in the fields, the indifferent English government, enough food to feed double the population going out from the land and across the sea; a desperate people. The numbers are terrible. More than a million of the eight million people in Ireland died of starvation and illness. Another three million managed to get out of the country during the next fifteen years, but a hundred thousand of them died on the way.

Six of my eight great-grandparents lived through the famine. When they came to America, they must have been ashamed — as if it had been their fault that they'd had no food, no schooling, that the clothes they wore were torn and filthy. One of my great-aunts shook her head. "I'm a Yankee," she said. "Whoever told you I was Irish?"

My uncle held up his hand when I

asked. "You don't want to know," he said.

And so the family stories that might have been handed down from one generation to the next were never told. But I did want to know. I longed to know. I told myself that my beautiful Irish grandmother Jennie would have told me what she had heard from her mother. But she died before I was born, and all I have of her is a picture that hangs in my dining room and a soft pink shawl.

Year after year I traveled to Ireland, to that lovely green country. "Tell me," I asked distant relatives. "Do you know anything about it?"

I asked people I met: "Please, tell me anything."

I collected in my mind every single shred of what they told me. One man waved his hand across the fields, saying, "If only we'd had a little help from the British government, we'd have all survived." He smiled at me. "You'd have been an Irish girl living in Drumlish, instead of a girl from New York."

I saw huge walls that had been built around the estates so that no Irishman could climb and take food for his children.

I saw mounds of earth where those who

had died were buried without markers.

I listened to a wonderful Irish professor with the same name as mine tell me what she knew, and I saw the memorials in Roscommon and Cobh. . . .

And then in my mind I saw an old woman named Anna who wouldn't leave me. I saw a girl named Nora who looked like the picture I have of Jennie, with her dark hair and freckles. I saw the chances those Irish women of the 1800s must have taken to survive, their strength and their luck.

At last, I ran my hands over the rough walls of my great-grandmother's house, the house that was there during the famine, and I walked up the road and tied a piece of my jacket sleeve to the tree over Patrick's Well. I tucked a manuscript page between the rocks and made my wish. "Let me tell it the way it must have been. I want my children and grandchildren to know. I want everyone to know."

I went home then to write under Jennie's picture, with her shawl around my shoulders.

Patricia Reilly Giff
January 2000